The Reflective Cause

Tamara Rose Blodgett

THE REFLECTIVE CAUSE

Book Two: The Reflection Series

ISBN: 150785420X

ISBN-13: 9781507854204

Cover art: *Phatpuppyart.com*

Editing suggestions provided by: *Red Adept Editing*

Dedication

Beth Hill

You mean so much to me~

Directives of The Cause

Fourth: *Reflect only when unobserved*
Fifth: *Protect the young*
Sixth: *Take life only in defense of another*

1

Beth

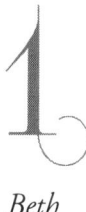

Waves lap gently at Beth's feet as she wades into the cold, unfeeling water that is her portal to Papilio.

Merrick's hand grips hers as the water level rises to Merrick's shins and just above Beth's knees.

Beth shivers at the contrast of warm air and cold water.

She glances over her shoulder at the unforgiving faces of Reflectives who've never accepted her.

The very thing they loathe about Beth is now their collective redemption.

Her ability to jump is all that matters.

The lake stills in the breezeless heat of high noon. Blood and grime covers everyone. Beth's jaw still throbs from the hit she took in the illegal fighting ring on Sector One.

Ryan is nowhere to be found. And searching for that loose end is not as important as returning to reclaim the ravaged Papilio. Merrick has not elaborated on the severity or type of compromise, and Beth's speculations have run rampant.

At least a hundred Reflectives converge behind her and Merrick; their weight presses on her shoulders.

They wait.

Beth steadies herself, centering her energy for the jump, trying not to think of the *why* and *how* to come.

I just want home.

"*Salire verum*, Beth," Merrick encourages.

Jump true. Beth nods, not trusting her voice because the heat from her body makes her feels as if she's on fire—as though she always has been.

Merrick's hand convulses in her own. In her peripheral vision, Beth sees his head tip back, mouth agape as he groans against the rush of warmth created by her reflective energy.

The heat ripples away from her as if she were a thrown stone, sending shock waves of fire-tinged water behind her across the surface of the lake. A soft chorus of acceptance, revelry, and want surrounds her as the Reflectives are uplifted by her jump.

Home.

She and Merrick land in perfect synchronicity then jog for several meters before slowing.

Merrick spins Beth into his arms, burying his face in her hair. He pulls her more tightly against his frame.

"I thought I'd lost you."

No, Beth thinks, *I lost me.*

Merrick pulls away, scrutinizing her face. "Beth, we're here—in Papilio. You're safe."

Beth was safe with Slade, too. She covers her face with her hands as a choking sob bursts from her at the traitorous thought of the Bloodling. How can she think of her captor as anything but someone she survived?

Because I can still feel his lips on mine.

Beth covers her mouth to keep the words from forming.

"Wait? What is this?" Merrick gently removes her hands, and thumbs away the wetness.

"I have abandoned the Bloodling."

Merrick's expression darkens. "The one who fought Reflective Ryan?"

She nods. "Yes. He saved me—protected me. I don't know what has happened to him."

Merrick steps away, surveying her miniscule expressions. "I'll tell you what happened—he and Slaver Dimitri must find a new battalion of people to abuse. We have brought our fellow Reflectives home, Beth."

Instantaneous rage fills her. Merrick doesn't know what happened on One. Only Slade knew. And how did she repay him? She left him to die.

Beth doesn't dare touch the memories of Reflective Ryan and how he'd almost killed her in the ring.

She walks away from Merrick as chaos ensues all around them and Reflectives begin running to The Cause headquarters.

"Wait!" Merrick bellows, gripping Beth's upper arm. She jerks it away.

He easily swings her to face him, his face stern. "Beth, hang on. It's volatile right now. I've not had time to recount…on what Papilio has become."

Two dozen Reflective warriors pause, their heads whipping in Merrick's direction.

Merrick's words are grim as he addresses them. "Use caution. We were unable to locate Reflective Ryan while on One." His eyes land purposefully on each face. "He could be anywhere. Iver and Quaker are in cahoots with him, as well as up to a dozen others—from what Calvin and Kennet report. Be vigilant."

Several people nod, their eyes moving curiously over Beth.

Some expressions are neutral…others, not so much. Merrick opens his mouth to add something, clearly thinks better of it, then clamps his lips.

"Go!" he commands harshly.

The Reflectives scatter, and Merrick wraps a strong arm around her shoulders. "Beth," he says, cupping her chin. Pale gray eyes storm into hers and Beth blinks back sudden tears. She feels nothing but pain. She's in control of nothing. Her life as she's known it is over.

"Do *not* feel guilt, Beth. You were dragged to One by Ryan, from underneath my nose. Thrust into a world the likes of which you've never seen. The Bloodling proved honorable. But"—Merrick dips down to catch her gaze—"a male of that integrity would never hold you responsible for his safety." His eyes thaw. "You are female, Beth.

She jerks away, stomping off with crossed arms.

Female! Gah!

Merrick chases her down.

Beth doesn't even know where she's going—she just has to move, get out of here. Her vision blurs, then Merrick's whirls her around, fingers digging into her shoulders. Eyes that were gentle seconds ago are hard pewter discs. "Beth!" Merrick shakes her gently. "I love you."

She hangs her head, trying to escape the intense revelation. "It's because I am your soul mate," she whispers.

Merrick tips her chin up, his thumb feathering her jaw. "No. Deep down, I always knew. But I resisted. I tried to *not* be your partner, remember? I tried to let you defend yourself against all comers. *You are Reflective*, a warrior as much as myself."

Beth's eyes search his. "Then why don't you trust me to be the keeper of my own safety?"

Merrick tugs her against him.

His heartbeat thuds against her cheek. "Because you are *my* female—you always were. When the timepiece slipped away, the gear of your position in my life fell into place as if I were an engine that wasn't running perfectly without you. I can no more choose another female than I could stop my next breath."

Beth squeezes her eyes shut against the truth of his words. They are real.

Devastating.

Merrick deserves her honesty. He went beyond the call of mere Reflective partnering. "I do not feel as you do, Jeb."

He strokes her hair. "I know. It will come."

Beth retreats from the comfort of his arms and looks into his face.

Jeb Merrick stares back, his golden brows pinched together.

"All I ask is that you entrust your well being to me. I must—I have to protect you. Please allow me to."

Beth opens her mouth to restate all that she understands to be true. Fifteen years of military training, her skills of blending in all sectors, her unparalleled jumping abilities—*Hades, I've just focused a jump for over a hundred fellow Reflectives*—that should be all the proof needed to show that she doesn't need protection.

But as Beth gazes up into Jeb's face, she knows she can't tell him those facts. Her training as a Reflective also made the significance of the soul mate bond absolutely clear: it is unbreakable. When a Reflective finds a mate, that person knows it with the deepest fiber of his or her being. It was not happenstance—but providence.

Beth nods. She won't swim upstream in this. "Yes." Jeb would not take no for an answer; he's incapable. Leaving her to her own devices would go against his every instinct.

Jeb draws her to him, and she looks up as he looks down. He threads his long fingers into her undone hair. He grips the strands, tightening almost to the point of pain, and reverently kisses her forehead.

Hot kisses slide like satin over her face as Beth closes her eyes, accepting the intimacy, letting it move her.

With a quiet moan of consent, she winds her fingers around his thick neck, and Jeb lifts her against his body, kissing her closed eyes and her cheeks.

When he finds her mouth, she opens it to his gentle demand, and their tongues meet in a twining embrace of desperation and rightness.

Warmth bleeds from the kiss, shooting sparks of tingling need and uncertain desire through Beth's limbs. She hangs loosely in Jeb's embrace.

A throat clears and Beth gasps, completely disorientated in the moment.

She has never kissed anyone before.

No male from her world would have her.

Now this male will have no one else.

"Can't you two figure out more important things to do? God, chill out with the hump fest." Jacky cocks a sandy eyebrow.

Beth blinks, sliding down the front of Jeb's body, feeling his hardness, her face flushing like a coal from the fire.

Beth opens her mouth to rebuke him—and can't manage it. Instead of the nearly thirteen-cycle youth Beth remembers, Jacky looks like a young man. His appearance causes Beth's shame to burn more brightly than ever.

He caught us making out in the middle of a revolt.

However, Jeb glares at Jacky. "You have the worst timing of any creature in any sector."

Jacky grins, stabbing a thumb at his chest. "Creature? Hmm..." He palms his chin and gives a slow nod. "I dig that."

"How—" Beth chokes, feeling her face reignite. "How are you?" Beth sweeps a hand toward Jacky, who is now suddenly a Three teen on the verge of manhood.

Jacky preens, spinning in a languid circle. "You can say it." He makes a show of blowing hot air against his fist and shining it on a worn-out Reflective uniform. "I look *hot*." He waggles his eyebrows.

Beth blanches, clearing her throat. "Uh..." She takes in the six-feet tall, strapping, and suddenly muscled young man then manages to sputter, "You look very grown up now."

"So awkward," Jacky chimes, "but that's cool. There's plenty of chicks who are going to dig my swag."

Beth ignores him. "Ah." She turns to Jeb. "How is *this* possible?"

Merrick tears his fingers through his messy hair. "Five years have passed since our mission."

Beth blinks, stumbling back.

Jeb's strong hands arrest her momentum. "Shhh, it's all right."

Adrenaline kicks through her system. "Fuck that!" Beth screams, swinging wildly out of his grip.

Jacky makes a contemplative noise. "Remember what that twat waffle Ryan said at my place?" Jacky asks.

Beth backs away from them both. She knows how long she's been gone: *Days*.

Not years.

Jeb scowls warily at Jacky, who is eyeing Beth. "Jacky—cease that."

He shrugs, flinging his palms wide. "Nope. I'm going to do *me* all the way, Jeb."

Jeb stalks toward Jacky, who wisely retreats, matching the older man's steps.

"Wait," Beth says, holding her hands up. "Jacky, shut up. I'm thinking."

Jacky smirks. "Think away. Papilio is falling down around our heads, but let's stand around choking the chicken while we *think it out*." He nods as though answering himself. "Yeah, I'm on board with that plan." He rolls his eyes.

Jeb ignores Jacky, walking back to where Beth stands.

"Jeb—tell me what has happened in five years?"

His eyes fall to the side, and Beth draws nearer, gripping his biceps, her fingertips clenching against the roughness of his uniform. "Tell me."

He covers her hand fisting his shirt.

"You will not like it."

Their eyes lock.

"Now *that's* a no-shitter," Jacky pipes up in the background.

He's right.

Beth didn't like it. Not one bit.

2

Merrick

Jeb scrubs his face, frowning at the stubble peppering his jaw. Every nerve he possesses is raw and exposed.

Beth is his soul mate. And that one thing, so pivotal—so unavoidable—has irrevocably changed their relationship. She knows there is no way Jeb would claim her unless it were so.

None.

Her status of soul mate is not predicated on whether Papilio is on its ear from a tyrannical regime of perverted Reflectives.

Some prejudices run bone deep. His claim of her should be proof that Beth is pure enough to warrant the tie of a Reflective.

But those who hold to the old beliefs will try to make their lives miserable, whichever regime rises from the ashes after the last five years.

However, Jeb has too many current variables to worry about. His first order of business must be protecting Beth—against her express will. Yes, she'd conceded to the idea that she would allow his watch care. But in practice?

Never.

Jeb glares at Jacky. He should be returned to Three.

He'll never go. Not as long as Madeline DeVere is unaccounted for.

"Jeb," Beth calls gingerly, and he swings to face her. "We need to go to the TCH."

Jeb sighs, planting his hands on the hips of his dirt-encrusted uniform.

"I say negative to that, Jasper," Jacky says in crisp mockery, cocking his head toward TCH. "There's some shit going on. And I'm not down with whatever that nasty little catastrophe is."

Beth's face scrunches with determination, and Jeb knows Jacky has lost before he does.

Jacky ignores Beth. "What I really wanna do is get Maddie and get the fuck outta Dodge. This place—old utopia? Not so cool anymore. Reflectives turned into pimps, killing each other. And One was *fun*, just sayin'."

Jeb strides to Jacky, who remains where he stands. Jeb pokes his chest and Jacky stumbles back a half meter. "Thank you so much for your enlightenment."

"Jeb!" Beth shouts.

Shove.

Jacky staggers again then roars like a lion and attacks Jeb.

Jeb is a trained Reflective, but he's never had a Three, whose not quite a man, come after him, and he's utterly unprepared.

The boy feints to the left, and Jeb deflects automatically with a raised forearm.

Jacky takes Jeb's forearm in both hands, sinking his teeth into it as if it were his favorite drumstick.

Jeb howls, moving to backhand him.

Beth is suddenly there, hanging off Jeb's arm.

She jabs Jeb in the ribs with a perfectly executed strike, playing his ribs like a keyboard. Jeb grimaces and slaps Jacky, sending him flying.

Jeb whirls to Beth, a vein in his forehead pulsing in time to his rage.

Beth bounces from foot to foot, her fists raised beside her jaw. Waiting.

Jeb's anger leaks away, shame taking its place. His arms drop to hang loose by his sides. "I would *never* harm you."

She straightens, dropping her fists. "There's more to harm than using your fists, Jeb."

He looks at a bleeding Jacky on the ground. His Adam's apple makes a painful plunge inside a throat gone dry.

"I'm sorry—he—I—" Jeb begins.

"Shut up, Jeb," Beth says, turning her back on him. She walks to Jacky and offers a hand.

He slaps his palm inside hers, and she lifts him easily. Jacky's eyes widen as he bounces to a standing position. "Stronger than you look, Jasper."

A vague smile is gone from her face almost as soon as it appears.

"Beth," Jeb says, reaching for her.

"Jeb," she shoves her matted hair behind an ear, "I can't do *us* right now. I have to see where Rachett is. *If* there's a Rachett." Beth sucks her bottom lip into her mouth. "And you need to control your emotions."

The warmth Jeb feels for her swells unbearably inside him at the small gesture of pain. Eyeing Jacky, Jeb ignores Beth's dismissal.

"I apologize."

Jacky spits blood. "Whatever, ya fuckin' hothead."

Jeb's jaw clenches and he keeps walking. When he reaches Beth he pulls her into his arms. "I'm so sorry. I didn't want to lose my temper. We were wracked with thoughts of our fellow Reflectives on One—you were there with only a pack of Bloodlings as protectors, and Ryan gunning for your death. I haven't had a moment's respite from my fear over your safety."

Beth relaxes slightly. "I think I liked it better when you didn't like me, Merrick."

"Jeb," he corrects, hating the sheen of tears he has put in her eyes.

Beth places her palms against his chest, allowing her forehead to rest lightly against his thudding heartbeat. "Don't touch Jacky again, or I'll have to kick your ass.

He's not the enemy here. He's an orphan, for Principle's sake."

Jeb cups the back of her skull, his regret drumming between them. "Okay," he answers simply.

"How about a god-blessed shower in this place?" Jacky asks.

They smile, breaking away.

Jacky is always himself.

Some things remain constant, Jeb thinks.

His smile fades as he realizes how little has.

"Stay within sight, Beth," Jeb instructs quietly.

"Jeb." Beth sighs in clear frustration.

"Humor me," he answers, swinging his gaze to hers.

After a handful of seconds, she nods.

Jeb stops short, and Jacky jerks to the tips of his toes to avoid a collision.

"What the hell?" Jacky whispers.

The beautiful sculpture of a shimmering bronze swarm of butterflies has been dismantled. Their bodies lie on the ground like wounded corpses.

Beth covers her mouth as Jeb silently takes her hand.

As they walk to the entrance, Jeb takes in the stains of blood where he beat Quaker using a dose of Reflective trickery.

TCH is effectively deserted. Jeb carefully looks for others, and does see some of the many Reflectives Beth helped jump to their world.

But the female Reflectives are nowhere to be seen.

The money taker's station is upturned; Papilio currency floats like spent garbage in a breeze that whips through, whistling its despair at the leavings of their antiquated city.

Grief strangles Jeb's chest. He hadn't allowed emotions to touch him when he, Calvin, and Kennet made their plan for the retrieval of so many, but now the stark consequence of his new reality was biting him in the ass, as Jacky would say.

Jeb turns, hunting for the young man, and finds him caressing a fractured marble pillar that had stood unmolested for one thousand years.

But it's Beth's grief that tugs at him without mercy. She shakes off his comfort and strides forward, her eyes ping-ponging across every surface as though the answer for the dissenters' debauchery might spring forth.

"How could they—devalue The Cause?" she asks to no one.

"Beth..." Jeb walks to where she stands, her hands cupping her elbows, her face a mask of betrayal. Raw pain bleeds from her every feature.

"Let's get out of here. Go back to our domiciles and get..." Jeb offers.

"What? Supplies?" Jacky spins, torqueing his body to one side. "Yeah, I'm seeing lots of regular stuff happening.

We're gonna have to go back to the 'hunt and gather' bullshit."

Beth looks between the two of them. "He might be right. Did you?" Horror dawns over Beth's face.

"What?" Jeb asks in alarm, scanning the perimeter. He sees no threats.

"My butterflies!" Beth cries.

Then she runs.

What butterflies? "Beth!" Jeb roars, tearing after her.

He yells to Jacky, "Follow!"

"Yes, sir, your majesty!" Jacky says.

Jeb doesn't have time to bludgeon Jacky again, however tempted he is.

Beth leaps at the first mirrored streetlamp solar panel she can.

"*No*—Beth!" Jeb bellows.

They might not be stable. Jeb has no way of knowing. Yet that unknown potential doesn't keep him from jumping after her.

Jeb turns, slapping his hand around Jacky's forearm. His mossy-green eyes bulge, then Jeb is tearing them forward, leaping into a fifty centimeter square then into the next.

The leap-frogging method feels natural to Jeb. However, it has the opposite effect on Jacky, who begins to vomit after only three jumps.

"Pudwacker! This sucks!" He bellows in Jeb's ear as they hurtle the ten seconds between streetlamps.

Jeb winces. Sounds are amplified in transit.

They land in an ungraceful pile. Jacky bends over, and a third stream of bile shoots out of his mouth.

He'll live.

Jeb's eyes are already on Beth's domicile.

A door closes with a loud click as he watches. She's already inside.

"Come on," Jeb says, heading toward the shared domicile.

"Are ya okay, Jacky? Do you have jumper's sickness? Can I get you something to take away your *fucking* nausea!" he screams at Jeb's back.

Jeb turns. "I don't have time for your self-pity. We must find Beth and get sustenance. In that order."

Jacky stares at him. After almost a full minute, he comments, "You're a jackass. You were a helluva a lot more fun when you didn't have a soul mate and you had to use my words. Now, you're just a stuck-up, Latin-speaking pain in my ass."

Jeb groans. *I don't have time for this!*

He stalks directly to the door and rips it open. Jacky jogs to catch up and manages to jam a sneakered toe inside the door before it closes.

Jacky fights to open the heavy door.

Jeb has to return and open it for him. He throws the heavy gallery-height door wide and it smacks into the wall.

Small flakes of plaster float to land at their feet, and Jacky steps away from Jeb.

First sentient thing he's done.

"Exactly how strong are you guys?" Jacky asks, scooting through the doorway and studying the steep staircase.

The door swings shut behind him with a clank.

"Four times stronger than the average human male on Three," Jeb recites by rote.

Jacky hooks his fingers through the belt loops of the too-big Reflective uniform and blows his longish hair out of his eyes. "Well, you're a real winner, beating the shit out of an almost eighteen-year-old Three. I never had a chance, ya douche."

Principle, help me.

Jeb turns. "Hear me. This"—livid, he swings a palm around the tight space of the foyer—"is entirely too much for me. I'm hungry, tired, and dirty. And my soul mate is not within sight. In the economical words of your sector, I'm knackered."

Jacky's slow grin just pisses Jeb off more. He claps Jeb on the back. "I gotcha, ya big sloppy turd. When things go to hell, you can't keep a stiff upper lip."

"What?!" Jeb brays.

"I'm making fun of you, doofus. You're speaking like a Brit. You really screw up the linguistics, pal. But I'll forgive you if you can stop acting like a dickbag for, like"—he looks up, cupping his chin—"two minutes." His eyebrows jump. "Think you can manage that?"

Jeb's not sure. If he were with anyone but Jacky, perhaps he might have.

Jeb turns on his heel and heads up a steep flight of stairs, going straight for a door with a number two on it.

"Can ya?" Jacky asks. "Because you're consistently pissing me off."

Jeb looks down at him.

Jacky's foot is poised on the first step as Jeb stands before Beth's locked door.

"I'll try," Jeb concedes through his teeth.

His gaze moves to the door. The silent compulsion to find and be with his soul mate is all-encompassing. He can't think of anything else.

Jeb depresses his thumb at the pulse dock beside the medieval door, and a low chime thrums through him and Jacky.

Beth tears open the door with such force, her hair lifts around her smiling face.

Jeb smiles automatically in return.

He's desperate for good news—anything to balance the desolation that sucks at their marrow.

"Maddie's here!" she squeals.

Jacky shoots forward like an arrow—into the waiting arms of a malnourished and frightened Three.

Jeb and Beth embrace and she whispers, "I think it might be okay, Jeb."

Jeb wouldn't go that far, but it's a start.

3

Slade

"Does she know, Bloodling?" the slaver's eyes narrow on him like a demon's.

"No. Do you not think if she knew, she would have been so willing to hop away with the Reflectives?" Slade asks the obvious.

Dimitri smirks.

Slade yanks his longish hair into its customary club at the base of his skull, wincing as he does.

That fuck Ryan damaged every surface of his body. Even bleeding out three nightlopers had not set things perfectly to rights. While Slade was busy recovering, Beth had jumped.

"We had an understanding, Slade. Did we not?"

Prick. "Yes," Slade hisses through fangs that sprout with his emotions.

"Tsk, tsk, Slade. Find the hopper. Bring her back to her home world."

Slade does not wish to hurt Beth Jasper. She has the bravest heart of any being he has ever encountered. He does not want to be the one who stops its beating.

He also does not wish Dimitri's threat against the Bloodlings to come to fruition. Their women have been captive since the great uprising after the death of Beth Jasper's mother.

The King of the Bloodlings, Slade's sire, had a warrior so fierce, he could kill twenty nightlopers with his own hands.

Then a female who reflected into the wrong sector compromised the warrior, Gunnar. Her death robbed him of his mind.

After the death of Slade's sire, Gunnar, Beth's father, was imprisoned.

Nothing consoles him, and he is too dangerous to set free.

With Slade's sire dead and their greatest warrior imprisoned, a slaver raid crippled the Bloodlings' force of the warriors.

Now Dimitri holds the strings to Sector One. He enslaves the Bloodling females while their race dwindles without the normal birthing of offspring.

Beth Jasper is the key.

If Slade wins her trust then delivers her to Dimitri, he will release the Blooding females and allow the dying race to flourish once more.

It's rudimentary.

Except, Beth will become Dimitri's queen. Part Bloodling, part Reflective, she is a perfect blending of the species. Their offspring would bring all three species together. A being who is part nightloper, Bloodling, and Reflective could travel to other worlds and dominate them one by one.

Dimitri's progeny would be unstoppable. A Reflective is a neutral vessel. A Reflective who is also Bloodling is two thirds of the way to being a perfect catalyst for the domination of the thirteen sectors.

Beth can free the Bloodling race forever.

But Slade's heart and mind will fail him with that choice. He clenches his fists, casting his eyes to the floor to hide the slide of his emotions across a face normally steeped in blankness.

Slade still remembers Beth's delicate body against his own—and her plea that Slade protect her from Ryan.

"Do not let him have me," she asked in a voice breathless with exhaustion.

It made Slade harden to think of her body. Her voice.

Everything that she is.

Slade resists the truth, for it is too damning. He wants Beth Jasper for himself, to breed her and keep her as his mate.

"Will you do it, prince? Will you fetch the hopper for me?"

Slade's chin jerks up. He carefully schools his expression to nothingness once more. Though Dimitri's nostrils flare hard to catch the scent of Slade's emotions, he will be unable to.

Slade is of royal blood, after all, and has a fine ability to scent-mask.

Dimitri watches him closely.

Slade leans back in a hard chair, and it groans under his weight. "Of course."

His eyes narrow at Slade. "Do not fuck her, Slade, or I will cut off your prick."

Slade's heart speeds, but he sneers, "Is that *all* you think of?"

Dimitri tilts his chin, and golden eyes that speak of his lion heritage seem to debate the ceiling of the lair. "Mostly."

"You are pathetic," Slade says, fantasizing about beheading Dimitri with his bare talons.

A smile ghosts the slaver's lips. "You can hide most emotions, but lust is the strongest of all, and you *reek* of it, my friend."

Slade stills, and Dimitri leans forward. "I would love to feel flattered, presuming you wish to pierce me with your sizeable attributes, but I have it on good authority, you fancy your sex from the fairer persuasion. So it is just the *mention* of Beth Jasper that gets you salivating like a rutting bull."

Slade can't deny it, but he clamps down on his rage, and his apparent desire for Beth, with an effort. Casually, he leans back in the wooden chair, lacing his hands behind his head, and lifts a shoulder. "She is tempting, I'll admit, but she's just a hopper."

Dimitri steeples his fingers beneath his chin. "Just a hopper?" He shakes his head, a sound of disbelief escaping his lips in a soft hiss. "This is where you stumble upon your words, Bloodling."

Slade remains silent, continuing his feigned nonchalance.

"She is so much more than the sum of her genetics. Beth Jasper is the key to your females. She is the ultimate manipulator of Gunnar—the greatest war strategist of the millennium. Do you not think if he *knew* his union had produced a daughter, he could not be controlled?"

The legs of his chair slam brutally against the stone floor, and Slade points at Dimitri. "You said you wished to have the Reflective female for your own sexual depravity. Not as a tool to manipulate a grief-crazed Bloodling warrior."

Dimitri nods happily. "Yes, and do not belittle my intentions toward the lovely Beth. She will be treated as the queen she is. But why not put a cherry on top of the lovely cake of opportunity?" He folds his hands, letting them fall on the surface of his ornate desk of stone.

"Beth Jasper is a Reflective warrior. She will *not* submit."

Dimitri's lips thin into a wicked grin, and he spreads his palms. "Now where is the fun in that?"

Slade feels as though his head will explode. He must leave or kill Dimitri, but not until the negotiations are over.

"You will release half of our women before I travel to take the hopper."

Tiny frog, Slade's mind whispers. He ruthlessly shoves the endearment aside.

Beth Jasper is a means to an end. He can't let their shared blood, or desperation for a female of his own kind, sway him. His duties to his people must take precedence.

Dimitri inclines his head. "Will your men be able to stand the feminine flesh served up once more after such a long hiatus?"

Slade stands, clearing his throat in disgust. He's had enough. "If you had not kept our females from us for two decades, there would be no concern to voice."

A sly smile overtakes Dimitri's face.

"However, unlike the nightlopers, we do not rape and abuse our females."

Dimitri's smugness vanishes. "We do not harm our females, as a rule."

Their hate-filled gazes lock.

Neither mentions the catastrophe of the faction of criminal nightlopers who would have gang-raped a group of barely grown nightloper females for sport.

If it had not been for Slade and a few other Bloodlings who were in the right place at the right time, it would have gone into the archival history of a brutal and unregulated race.

"Enough!" Dimitri bellows into the sharp acoustics of his den.

Slade rounds the corner of the stone table, and their chests meet.

"However it occurs—it does," Slade says. "The Bloodlings will not be rapists of their own females. Send the females to our coven—unharmed, and you have a deal."

Slade steps back, arms loose and ready in case Dimitri finds a purpose for the meeting other than demonstrating his control over Slade.

Dimitri's face flushes a dull red underneath golden skin. He's majestic in his rage, but all Slade can see is the evilness of his machinations against anyone outside of himself.

"It was happenstance that Beth Jasper fell into our laps," Slade reminds him, breaking into the taut moment.

Dimitri whirls away from him. "Then it is most fortuitous for your precious females that she did."

Slade tenses. "Did you crush the spirits of our women, you horrible fuck?"

Dimitri turns, a sliver of his face lit in profile from the poor lighting of the den. "What do you think, Bloodling?"

Slade grinds his teeth and walks out, giving Dimitri a hard shoulder swipe as he passes.

Bastard.

Slade's stomach is tight with anxiety as he approaches the cell holding Gunnar.

Honoring this warrior is the very worst promise Slade made at his sire's deathbed.

Full Bloodlings are a vicious group. Descended from a race of Blood Singers and pure vampire from Sector Seven, they are a perfect mix of predator and supernatural. Some Bloodlings even retain Angel's blood from the Singers royal line.

Not Slade.

And apparently, not Gunnar.

Those with Angelic blood did not advance as warriors unless pitted against the demonic. Now, in a battle between those two species, they would be well-suited.

Slade walks with purpose through the dimly lit winding stone corridor of the guarded prison of the Bloodlings. Only half the cells are filled.

Slade takes the smallest measure of pride that under his stewardship, his people have a moral code to some degree. His jaw clenches as he thinks of the returning females, many of whom Dimitri has broken. *Who's to know if they will be resilient enough to take mates who are meant to protect them?*

After passing ten empty cells, Slade comes to the last.

Gunnar heaves his body up and down, nose nearly scraping the floor as his powerful arms push his stiff body away from the ground. His toes and hands are the only parts of his body touching the stone floor.

Slade stands stiffly, not sure how to begin his revelations.

"Speak!" Gunnar barks as he lowers himself.

Slade is not one to fluster easily, but this insane Bloodling fills him with anxiety.

It could be because Slade has plans to figuratively fuck his daughter. No matter how much he justifies the cause as a noble one, Slade is ashamed.

"Gunnar," Slade begins with quiet respect.

The warrior bounces up from his prone position on the stone floor, dusting off his hands and strides to the bars.

His gray skin is so fair, it mimics the palest stone. Gunnar is intimidating, for he is the largest of Bloodling kind. Almost seven feet of hardened warrior with nothing but time to hone his body and ravage his intellect with vengeful grief makes a formidable presence.

Slade stays out of reach, his heart galloping. He knows what he must do and hates the thought of torturing this warrior further.

In this moment, Slade deeply loathes his life.

Eyes like black water regard him. Hair of a matching color is bound in a tight band not unlike Slade's. He looks so much like the masculine version of Beth, it tightens Slade's guts.

Gunnar cocks his head, nostrils flaring. "Slade, speak."

"I must—" Slade swallows against his shame. "I must ask that you jump me to Sector Ten."

Gunnar flinches, his hands clenching into fists. "Do not mention Ten to me again if you want to live."

Slade nods, holding his breath.

What he does now he does for his people.

An exhale rushes out of him. "I have news."

"News that makes your pulse race, your pupils dilate, and cold sweat form on your body, Slade?" Gunnar's voice has dropped to mercenary levels.

"Yes," Slade answers.

Gunnar's dark eyes narrow with pure distrust, his crazed features constantly scanning for anything reflective.

He would need only the finest particle of reflective material to escape. Gunnar's talent makes the Reflectives of Sector Ten look like toddlers.

"What news?" he asks slowly. He crosses his arms, inky eyebrows jerk in disbelief.

"Your daughter," Slade says softly.

Gunnar's face screws up in lines of hate. "I have none, fool. My mate was murdered. Do you not remember!?" he roars, sending spittle flying. The ceramic bars are poisoned, but he grabs them with his powerful hands anyway, forcing his face between the bars. His flesh begins to burn as though touching acid in reaction to the poisonous coating.

Slade sighs, pulling out a small circle of coated elastic, and brings it up between their faces.

Gunnar releases the bars with a hiss, flinging his smoking hands. "What is this?"

Slade places it between Gunnar's two fingers.

An inky hair clings to the figure eight of the twisted material. Gunnar snatches it from between Slade's fingers.

Never looking away, he brings it to his nose and scents of it deeply.

Gunnar's face slips to rage as his fingers close around Beth's hair band.

"Where. Is. She?" he roars, grabbing the bars once more.

Slade hangs his head. "She is at Ten—Beth Jasper is a Reflective."

Gunnar backs away from the bars and sits hard on the foldaway cot fixed against the wall.

His head droops into the palm not gripping the hair band. "As Lucinda was."

Slade nods solemnly.

Gunnar leaps up, heading for the bars of his cell.

His mouth opens, teeth snapping. Venom from mature and lethal fangs drips, sizzling like acid as it falls.

"I want to claim my child."

Of course he does.

That's what Dimitri's counting on to force his cooperation.

"I have been chosen to acquire her, and return her to her rightful sector."

Gunnar's fangs slide away, and he studies Slade. "You want me to reflect you to Ten?"

Slade nods.

Gunnar shakes his head. "Give me a drop of water, and I will seek my own blood."

The lie comes with difficulty, made easier by the threat against the Bloodlings' womankind. "Dimitri will kill her if I do not do this in secret. If you go, he will see your leaving as invitation for her death."

He has my mother and sisters. Slade feels helpless. The nightlopers number three times as many and breed as litters. There are no better options than this terrible one.

Gunnar nods, palming the hairless skin of his jaw.

"Will you?" Slade asks, his held breath like fire.

Gunnar lifts his chin. "I shall."

Slade walks away, taking the image of Gunnar's violence and his exploit with him.

4

Merrick

Jeb watches Beth's joy overtake her from the simple fact that Maddie is alive.

It's no small thing that the papiliones have somehow managed to survive.

The lights attached to the huge hand-hewn wooden beams bisecting Beth's ceiling no longer glow. Electricity fueled by solar power doesn't appear to be regulated any longer.

But the butterflies don't mind the dark, and they swarm to greet their disheveled and haggard group.

An especially large butterfly swoops down as Beth reaches a finger toward its velvety wings. It lights on her fingertip and Beth croons, "There, there, Sampson. I do adore you." Beth tilts her face, and the butterfly's wings whips softly against her cheek.

Jeb would like to revel in the reunion but more pressing things beckon.

He leaves Jacky and Maddie to embrace and sweeps the house. Something Beth didn't think to do. Her lack of awareness speaks to the shock of the last few days.

Jeb's eyes move everywhere, noting filth in the corners and half eaten food stuffs strewn around a kitchen without water.

Jacky moves to turn on a light. "Do not!" Jeb hisses and the boy's hand stalls.

"What? It's darker than pitch, Merrick."

Jeb nods within the gloom. "Yes, so let's not announce our presence."

"Jeb's right, Jacky," Beth says. "However..."

I thought too soon. Jeb crosses his arms.

"I have a back-up system. We could implement the pulse code, and while the water is heating, we could find something to eat."

Maddie's lip trembles before she swiftly tucks it inside her mouth. Dirty tracks from her tears line her face. "There is nothing to eat."

"Damn," Jeb says quietly.

"Not true." Beth smiles.

Jeb takes another look around the pathetically old-fashioned abode and smirks. There's not a crumb to be had. He shoots her a pointed look of disbelief.

She gives a small shrug. "I have a pulse-hydrator."

Fabulous. Jeb's mouth falls open, and Beth walks by, poking him in the gut as she passes. He catches her finger, raises her palm to his lips, and presses a soft kiss in its center.

Sampson the butterfly rises and flies to the rafter, where it perches on the glossy wood, seeming to observe them.

"Jeb," Beth begins.

Jeb can't help it; he pulls her against him and presses her head into his chest.

Maddie's face registers her shock. "What—what've I missed?" She looks first at Jeb then Beth.

Jacky answers, "A shit ton. First, we got our asses handed to us in our world. My folks were murdered."

Eyes round, Maddie slaps her hands over her mouth. "Oh my God, Jacky. I'm so sorry," she whispers through her fingers.

Jacky takes her hands, tugging her to the couch. They sit down slowly, and he looks into her eyes. "It was Chuck all along, Mad. He was the one who killed Chase and made it look like a car accident."

Maddie snatches her hands back.

Jeb and Beth loosen their hold, turning their attention to the Threes.

She shakes her head. "No—he couldn't."

Jacky nods thoughtfully. "He *totally* did. Admitted it to me, killed my folks on the anniversary of Chase's death. Then he took Beth and worked her over pretty good."

Maddie looks at Beth, and she lowers her head. Adrenaline shoots through Jeb's system at just the memory of what he saved her from—what it could have turned into.

Maddie's chin dips, and black hair slides forward to hide her face. "I'm glad he's dead."

Jacky rolls his eyes. "Well, duh."

Her head jerks up. She gives him a tentative smile then looks at Beth and Jeb. "But these guys. What—are they *together*, together?"

Beth sighs, stepping away from Jeb.

He aches from the distance, his jaw clenching. This soul mate stuff is all fine and dandy when the other half wants it, too.

Jeb's not so sure Beth does.

"Jeb has declared me his soul mate."

Maddie glances between the two of them. "Uh—you don't make it sound like great news, Beth."

Jeb lays his hand on Beth's nape, and just that simple contact soothes him. "When a Reflective's timepiece has disintegrated, they are free to answer the call in one of the thirteen sectors for their other half."

"It's a big no-no for the 'other half' to be a Reflective," Jacky inserts.

"Jacky," Beth says sharply.

He tosses his arms in the air. "Just sayin'."

Maddie giggles. "So, why is Beth *the* girl?"

Jeb squeezes her lightly and drops his hand away.

Beth sighs.

"We've discovered that Beth has Bloodling genetics."

"They're a bad-ass vamp race who live in treehouses and shit." Jacky nods.

Jeb groans. "They are more than vampire. They are a mixed colony, descended from true vampires and extraordinary humans who possess pure blood. In certain cases, they possess angelic blood."

Maddie stares, her lips parting.

Jacky interjects, "None of those dudes were angels. Pfft—for real. I saw the fight between that clown Ryan and the big Bloodling dude. Nothing heavenly about that. Just a lot of ass-kicking."

"Slade," Beth whispers.

Jeb gives her a sharp look, trying to keep his anger in check. Something about Slade has her in knots, and Jeb wants to know what it is. *Did he hurt her?*

So help me, I will scour the earth if the Bloodling hurt a hair on her head.

"Anyways—" Jacky begins.

Jeb air slices a finger across his neck. "Enough." Jeb meets Maddie's deep-bluish-violet eyes. "Beth's lack of pure Reflective genetics is the exact component that's allowed her to call to me."

"So you two were working together all this time and didn't know she was your soul mate?" Maddie asks.

"The timepiece depresses the natural call," Beth explains.

Maddie looks at Beth. "What about you?"

"My timepiece is still operational."

Realization swarms Maddie's delicate features. "So he's digging you, and you're not feeling it?"

Jeb scrubs his head. "I'm hungry," he says, diffusing a hard discussion.

Maddie shakes her head. "Me, too, but how is this working? What if your soul mate is different?"

Jeb releases a harsh exhale, his patience vanishing. "In theory, when her timepiece degrades, she should reciprocate."

"Should—or will?" Maddie asks.

Jacky grins, leaning back against the couch and lacing his hands behind his head.

Jeb scowls at him but addresses Maddie's question. It's an important one. "Typically, a full-blooded Reflective will have a soul mate whose very being is linked to his own. Beth's blood is mixed and has allowed that. Pure Reflectives are not called to one another."

Jacky claps his hands together. "So here's the thing. Beth can have someone else besides perfect Jeb and they have to fight it out."

"You do *you*, Jacky," Maddie replies sarcastically, shaking her head.

Jacky shoots a mock gun at her with his fingers. "Uh-huh, that's it."

She rolls her eyes. "Sorry about him."

"Sorry? Look at me." Jacky splays his fingers on his chest.

Everyone stares. Jeb's eyes hold more than amusement.

Jacky meets his gaze. "Okay. I know you're pissed. But you have to admit, when has anything not gone Jeb Merrick's way?"

Beth strolls out of their little parlay and begins to pulse open a hidden safe in the wall.

Jeb steers his attention back to the boy. "I am Reflective. If you understood what that was, you would not ask such things."

"What I understand is you kicked everyone's asses everywhere you went, screwed all the hot Reflective chicks, and enjoyed a fat paycheck." He shrugs.

Jeb moves quickly.

Jacky leaps over the back of the couch and it tips, beginning to upend Maddie. Jeb soars over the back, using the backward momentum like a short step and scoops up Maddie to arrest her fall.

Jeb lands like a cat over Jacky, his feet planted on either side of Jacky's hips.

"Do not test me. I have no patience left."

"You're hurting me," Maddie says.

Jeb startles, realizing his fingers are digging into the girl.

"Apologies." He sets Maddie on her feet and helps Jacky up.

Jacky glares at him. "This is karma taking a chunk out of your ass. You are all soul-whatevered to Jasper, and she doesn't have the mojo on her end. So she's just seeing all the shit we all see, and she's not signing up. That's all."

Beth walks toward Jeb, and his breath catches at the sight of her. She's holding a bowl of fresh fruit, bread, and meats.

Jeb salivates, but the sadness in Beth's eyes robs him of hunger.

Maddie and Jacky grab the food and begin to dig in.

Jeb goes to Beth and tilts her chin up, mentally going over Jacky's unflattering tally of his traits. "Is anything they say true?"

Beth's smile is crooked. "Every bit."

Jeb scowls and turns from her. A soul mate is the one piece of happiness in the life of a Reflective, and he's been too selfish to see it.

Beth presses her forehead between his shoulder blades, putting her arms around his waist.

He's so startled, he doesn't move or breathe. His hands cover hers.

"It's all true. You're a selfish, domineering, man-whore who controls by fear and a healthy dose of intimidation."

Jeb's heartbeat stutters.

"You're also honorable, terrifyingly strong, and brilliant."

Beth comes around to his front, her hands trailing along his waist. Pebbling gooseflesh presses against his clothes.

Deep eyes regard him, and a cloud of dark hair has escaped her braids. Jeb cradles her face as she lifts her face to better meet his eyes.

The sounds of the Three's eating dims. Only her face crowds his vision. Her breaths are like music to his ears, her eyes eat every bit of him until he is nothing without her.

She speaks softly, and Jeb strains to hear, "You are the male who protected me when you hated who I was."

Jeb gives a hard choking swallow, never more close to tears than he is in this moment. "I never hated you."

"You are the man who loves me."

He grabs her hands. "I do."

She searches his eyes with a reticence born of pain and distrust. "Then give me time."

Jeb pulls her to him and Beth allows it.

He wraps his arms around her small body, feeling grateful to Principle she might be his—in a world that is no longer theirs.

5

Slade

Slade looks out over the water, where gentle ripples coast across the only reflective material on this side of the mountains of Sector One.

They must have water, or even this would be gone because of safe measures against jumping.

Slade shields his eyes, gazing up at the double moons. The larger overshadows the smaller. Slade has heard rumors that on Sector Three, they call an orange moon a "harvest moon."

On One, it is always the blood moon.

The bright orb indifferently regards the handful of Bloodling guards. Gunnar and Slade take in the effect of the setting sun as crimson creeps upon the great lake of One.

Slade will not be able to blend on Sector Ten, which is full to the brim with fair-complexioned papiliones. Slade's pearl-gray skin and eyes that appear pupil-less as well as his sheer mass will stand out. Bloodlings originate only on One. There is no precedent for their presence in any other sector. He'll be recognized as the alien he is before the first breath he takes on Ten.

That is why a magical camouflage has been devised. Unfortunately, veiling his true form comes at a price. He must give up his fangs and superhuman strength to assume the appearance of a papilion. He can't use what he is, or the covering of his Bloodling form will reemerge.

Slade glances behind him. Dimitri is accompanying him as insurance of a sort. After all, nightloper shifter magic rendered Slade's disguise. Slade never thought he would need anything from a brutal species who are the Bloodlings' sworn enemy.

But being held accountable for the safety of the Bloodling females has brought Slade's pride and moral compass to an all-time low.

He finds he'll do much to ensure the females' safety. *And Beth's.*

Gunnar asks, "Are you ready, Slade?"

Slade has no reflective abilities. Few on One do, and hopping is strictly prohibited. But some rare individuals—genetic throwbacks—have a streak of profoundly powerful reflective talent.

Slade's fingertips caress the hilt of his knives, all ceramic. Metal would not make the jump.

He nods, a breath of pure adrenaline leaking out of him.

"Yes."

Slade closes his eyes, tucking his arms tightly against his sides as he senses the guards behind him. His acute hearing can pick up each of their breaths.

Heat reaches for him like fingerless tendrils. Slade closes his eyes, hearing only the clanking of Gunnar's metal shackles.

Slade's eyes jerk open. Bloody diamonds litter his vision. The entire lake glitters as though rubies drench its surface.

An explosion of noise erupts behind him, but the sounds dim as the fine hairs on Slade's body rise in response to the heat and static of the jump.

Water splashes behind him, but Slade remains facing forward. Raised voices bellow.

Slade lifts his arm, which is opaque, like an image seen through dirty glass.

Blood roars in his ears, and ice pricks his exposed skin as fire laps behind the cold.

The silence is deafening, and the speed of transit spins his guts.

Slade is falling without landing. Then it's over as soon as it began.

Gunnar's reflective magic spits him out of the womb of the horrible tunnel of what feels like hades's passage.

Slade spins midair and lands hard. Because he is Bloodling and tree-bound for half his waking hours, he's accustomed to heights and dropping unexpectedly. Slade forces his body to loosen and rolls with the rough fall.

He somersaults a final time and bounds upright.

His vision triples. Slade gains his balance, but seconds tick by as he rights himself.

Finally, he's able to take stock of his immediate surroundings.

The air is drier than that of Ten, and the oppressive humidity of One is lacking here. Slade inhales deeply and coughs lightly, flexing his fingers. He turns at the waist, planting one hand at his lower back and swinging the other with the momentum of the motion. He reverses arms, swiveling away the aches and punishment of jumping.

How can the Reflectives stand to travel that way?

A stealthy movement captures his attention, and Slade spins, crouching low. Slade will always be instinctively violent—and defensive. He is a Bloodling.

His shock at the sight before him robs him of speech—and breath. Slade blinks, trying to clear his eyes, but his vision remains true.

Gunnar stumbles to gain his footing and falls on his rump. A great whoosh of breath escapes him, and he hisses in pain. His gaze lands on Slade, who finally sucks in much-needed oxygen.

"Come Slade, help me purge these wretched manacles from my body."

Slade opens and closes his mouth like a beached fish. He suddenly realizes why metal is not allowed in the jump.

The wrist and ankle shackles are now embedded in Gunnar's skin. The more prudent question is why Gunnar is here at all.

Slade retreats a step, folding his arms. "What have you done?"

Gunnar smiles despite his obvious agony. "You didn't really think I believed that nonsense about doing the honorable thing, did you?"

Actually, Slade had not really believed such a thing was possible.

Dimitri assured Slade that Gunnar could do nothing while bound in metal, almost as though he had fey blood.

But fey do not exist on One. That is another sector. Jumping requires that no metal be involved in the transition. *Any fool understands that.*

Traveling with metal speaks to Gunnar's desperation as well as his proficiency for jumping.

"Are you with me?" Gunnar asks.

Not really. Slade shakes his head, restating the obvious, "You are not camouflaged, and have manacles embedded inside your body."

Slade looks over the damage. The manacles present like partially manifested tumors at his wrists and ankles.

Gunnar grimaces. "You have knives. Don't be a weak kitten; slice them out."

Slade draws his dagger slowly.

His heart says to kill this insane warrior who is so buried in his own grief over the death of his Lucinda that he is unable to live in Bloodling society. *He's been incarcerated for twenty years—what life does he have anyway?*

Moving toward Gunnar, Slade casts a furtive glance around him. He sees nothing but the deepness of woods.

Satisfied with his superficial perusal, Slade carefully sets down his blade. Gunnar's deep eyes are shadowed pockets in his face, glittering darkly at his every move, and Slade knows to execute extreme caution.

He unhooks the belt from his weapons and hands it silently to Gunnar. He takes it, his chains rattling against the cuffs where they protrude from his flesh, and places the meaty part of the leather between his teeth. His fangs don't lengthen, probably due to anticipation of what's to come.

Slade marvels at Gunnar's bravery.

"Dimitri will seek your death upon our return," Slade states, the blade standing between them.

His eyes slim to slits. "Let him try," is Gunnar's garbled response.

Their gazes lock, and Gunnar nods in encouragement, sinking his teeth into the tooled leather belt.

Slade's weapon is as sharp as he remembers. Ceramic is somewhat lighter than metal, and he carries this with him always, never imagining it would be used for a hopping excursion or an impromptu surgery.

He excises the first manacle, a mess of sinew, blood, and muscle. Gunnar's forearm is left in ruins.

He groans, his eyes leaking tears of frustrated agony.

Slade moves to Gunnar's left arm, where the metal has less cruelly adhered. Only a thin coat of flesh covers the metal. It slices away easily, and Slade tosses the cuffs aside. They land loudly in a gore-soaked pile on the spongy forest floor.

Gunnar passes out during the incision at his second ankle. His great body eases, and the belt falls from his slack mouth.

Slade presses his blade to Gunnar's neck as he lies in the sleep of the grievously wounded.

Murdering him would be simpler.

He could end Gunnar's agony over Lucinda's death at the hands of the nightlopers.

Gunnar would never face Dimitri's punishment.

A thin red line appears beneath the serrated ceramic blade.

I cannot kill Beth's father.

Slade lifts the blade from Gunnar's throat, wiping blood and tissue from the smooth surface. He sheathes it on his weapons belt.

He takes a shaky inhale and attaches the belt to his body.

Gunnar's breathing comes even and deep. Slade watches as the Bloodling's body fills in the deep gouges caused by the metal.

Slade waits.

After an hour passes, Gunnar's eyes slowly open. His flesh has filled and repaired, but horrible butchering scars remain.

Slade and Gunnar gaze at each other for a handful of seconds.

"Blood," Gunnar croaks.

Slade nods. After that many wounds, it would take three nightlopers to set him to rights.

That was the number of Slade's victims after his battle with Ryan.

"We can't kill the papiliones. Our wounds are a signature to who we are."

Gunnar stands slowly, stretching in the same way Slade did when he first arrived. He swings in Slade's direction. "Agreed."

"We shall hunt, feed, and close their wounds as we put them in thrall," Gunnar says indifferently.

"Thrall may not work in this sector."

Gunnar smirks. "I've never met a Ten who could resist our gaze once captured in it."

"I don't have that benefit, Gunnar." Slade sweeps a hand over his altered form. "I will have to consume food as they do." Slade can't keep the abhorrent tone out of his voice.

Humanoid food tastes terrible. Only blood is truly satisfying. At least sunlight doesn't rule the Bloodlings. Slade can thank the ancient Blood Singers heritage for that at least. The inhabitants of the planet his long-ago ancestors called home would have called the Bloodlings a daywalking vampire.

But Slade has no desire to pay a visit to Seven. He is on Ten for one thing and one thing only.

Beth.

Unfortunately, his uninvited partner will see him dead if he discovers what Slade has planned for Beth.

Dimitri made good on his part of the bargain, having delivered half of the Bloodling females.

They were abused but technically alive.

Slade's body tenses, his hands closing into fists. A throbbing vein in his temple pulses with the memory of the females' treatment.

Now he must return with Beth to fulfill a bargain he struck in desperation.

Slade finds no good ending to any of this, no matter how many different ways he turns it over inside his mind.

Only after the tiny frog's return, will the remaining female Bloodlings be restored.

If it's the right thing for so many, why do I feel bereft at the thought of giving Beth over to the slaver?

6

Beth

Beth lets out a fairly decent belch and covers her mouth belatedly.

"Excuse me," she says delicately.

Jacky bursts out laughing, pointing the tines of his fork at her. "Nice."

Beth smiles. It's good to have some levity for once.

She ate practically her own weight in food. Beth's made ten trips in all to the food re-hydrator.

The re-hydrator had been her only concession to truly modern living, and she was never more thankful that she'd made it.

They'd been starving and so filthy, she couldn't stand her own smell.

Fortunately, they all smell the same.

Beth jumps up, wiping her mouth with the sleeve of the ruined uniform they found for her on One. "Cleansing," she announces decisively.

Maddie's face screws up. "I've been bathing at a nearby lake."

"For five years?" Beth asks, resting her foot against the wall.

She gives a grim nod. "I avoid everyone. Because—" Fat tears begin to track down her face as she looks at her hands. "Because *any* female…" Her chin rises, and her voice grows quiet. "Especially a woman with supernatural talent would be confiscated by The Cause."

Jeb walks toward her so fast, she flinches.

Beth tenses and steps away from the wall.

"That is *not* TC," he seethes.

Maddie backs away from his palpable rage.

Jeb paces away, hands pegged to his hips, jaw like granite. "That is a faction of derelict Reflectives who commandeered our headquarters while scheming a way to corrupt what it means to be Reflective."

Maddie recovers, seeming to understand that his anger is not directed at her. She gives a small shrug. "It is what it is, though. I came here, watched you and Beth jump, and then everything went to hell."

Jacky jerks his thumb in Maddie's direction. "Yeah, dude—what she said."

Jeb fumes silently, grinding his teeth.

"I think once we all get cleansed and get a few hours of rest," Beth says slowly, attempting to diffuse the emotional volatility, "everything won't seem so insurmountable."

Her eyes travel the group. "And if Maddie has somehow miraculously managed to survive in our absence, then we can take advantage of one more day of safety and much-needed recuperation."

Jeb sighs, his head drooping. "You're right, of course."

Jacky glares at him. "Show and tell can come later. The gut's full, I'm beat, and I need to grab a shower. Hell, even I can't stand myself." He snorts. "And that's sayin' something."

Jeb rolls his eyes. "Fine." Sweeping a palm toward the corridor, he says, "Ladies first."

Beth shoots a glance Maddie's way, and she stands from the couch. "We'll cleanse together—conserve water and heat."

"Good idea," Jeb remarks as Beth and Maddie move silently down the hall.

Maddie asks, "How are we going to even see?"

I've got that covered. A little smile hovers at Beth's lips, and Maddie offers a tentative one in return. "My old-fashioned ways are really going to save our butts." Beth sighs with relief when she opens the door and is greeted by her dusty but functional cleanser.

Beth leaves the door ajar, allowing moonlight to seep into the bathroom. By feel and the vague bluish-white illumination, Beth locates and sets the stumps of fat candles across a short bench meant for storing towels.

She throws the musty pile of towels to the floor and picks out two from the bottom. After a sniff, she wrinkles her nose. *At least the towels smell old rather than moldy.*

Beth hands one to Maddie, and her nose scrunches, but she says nothing.

The acrid fragrance of sulfur fills the space as Beth lights all five candles with matches retrieved from a toiletry drawer.

She opens the cabinet underneath the sink. A small dried-up bar of soap lies in a wicker basket along with a half bottle of shampoo.

She had a full cabinet's worth of both. Before. Perfumed toiletries and the length of her hair were Beth's only concessions to femininity.

"You were a little bit of a hygiene slut," Maddie admits with a giggle.

Beth smiles. "True." She gives Maddie a sidelong glance. "Lucky for you."

Maddie nods. "I actually stretched it as long as I could."

Beth looks critically at the girl. Maddie's hair falls to her mid-thigh, longer than the fashion of Papilio. After five years, Beth's midback-length hair has become too long.

"I know. You did great. I'm surprised without the rehydrator you didn't starve to death."

The silence stretches like pulled taffy between them, so many things left unsaid.

Then Beth closes the door, and they strip. Beth dumps the clothes into a pile to throw away.

"I guess I look terrible," Maddie says in an embarrassed voice.

Beth can count Maddie's every rib, and the girl's hipbones stick out like tent poles. She inhales deeply. "No.

You look like a woman who survived the unsurvivable. I don't think it matters how you look—only that you're alive."

Maddie begins to cry, covering her face with her hands.

Beth goes to her and takes her hands. "You're wasting water," Beth says gently. "We can't help what has happened. All we can do is restore TCH and hope the chaos of the last five years hasn't ruined things beyond fixing."

Beth dips her head, catching the taller woman's gaze. "Okay?"

Maddie nods. "I'm not crying because I'm sad, Beth."

Beth's brows draw together.

"I thought that I'd *never* see anyone else again, like I was surviving for nothing. I was on the last of my supplies here, worried about Ryan and his fucking goons coming by and nailing me—making me a whore like the others," she finishes in a whisper.

"Then we appeared," Beth interjects.

"Yeah," she says, wiping snot and tears from her filthy face. "Then you guys—you and Jacky—Jeb, walk in like a mirage in the middle of a desert. At first, I thought I'd finally lost it."

Maddie turns from Beth and walks into the cleanser, where she gives the faucet a hard jerk to the right.

The pipes groan in protest then finally splutter on.

"And then Jacky was there, looking older," she shakes her head, still looking away. "It doesn't seem real yet. I still feel like I need to hide." Her voice is soft, and Beth strains to hear her. "I'm still afraid," she adds.

Maddie turns and faces Beth, eyes large and shining with unshed tears.

The water hisses as it hits the tiles, and steam rises like mist between them.

The large cleanser is so big, both women fit inside easily. Beth holds up a wide-toothed comb of pure bone and makes a twirling motion with her finger. Maddie faces away, letting the spray from the cleanserhead rain down on the front of her.

Beth begins to comb the knots out of the other woman's matted hair.

"I'm afraid, too," Beth confesses. "But there's more of us than them."

"They're like ticks on a dog, Beth. They *liked* the violence—the control. They had all of Papilio held captive."

"Not Adlaine," Beth says with conviction, referencing her own quadrant. There's no way the people she grew up around would listen to a Reflective. Beth grins, thinking about it. Finally, their attitude might have helped.

"Yeah," Maddie says softly. "They held out until last year. Then Ryan's men burnt the quadrant to the ground and kidnapped all the women past menstruation age."

The comb clatters to the tile floor.

Maddie turns back to face Beth. Hot overspray soaks Beth's flesh. She can't swallow—or breathe.

Little girls that were barely women, taken to TCH to work as prostitutes...

"I'll kill them." Magic seems to build and seethe with her words as though taking on a life of its own, her words holding both power and weight.

Maddie's hand moves through the thickness of Beth's spoken promise, and she touches Beth's shoulder lightly.

"I know."

Whatever Beth's expression, it causes Maddie to drop her hand and retreat into the falling water.

"Every last one will die by my hand."

Maddie doesn't look afraid; she looks glad. A wide smile sits perched on her full lips. "I *knew* if you came back, you'd take them apart limb by limb."

Beth's lips curl. "That might be too quick for my taste."

They finish their shower in total silence. Beth counts it among the lengthiest showers of her life.

Beth assumes Maddie's thoughts are much the same as her own, though Maddie's are most likely mere dreams of vengeance.

However, Beth's does not dream; she plans.

Jeb smirks.

Jacky glares.

Beth barely holds back her laughter. "It's fine that Jacky doesn't want to shower with you Jeb."

"I'm not interested in males. Especially now," Jeb says, giving Beth a significant glance that instantly makes her uncomfortable, wiping all traces of humor from the moment. Her new status of declared soul mate and the uneasy climate they found upon their return to Papilio—she can't come to terms with any of it.

Jacky shrugs. "You guys can take long showers together here, but back on Three…there's no dropping the soap, if you catch my drift."

Jeb blinks.

Beth can't restrain her barking laugh and slaps a hand over her mouth.

Jeb turns to her with a frown.

"I'm sorry—it's so funny," she says.

"Beth, please."

"You're a serious dude. You need to chillax."

"And you're homophobic." Jeb's eyebrows cock, and he folds his arms over muscles that stretch beneath a T-shirt so snug, it's criminal. Beth simply doesn't have male clothes lying around her domicile. Both the men, if Jacky can be classified as such, had to make do.

Beth considers their wardrobe a form of comic relief.

"I'm cool with gay dudes, bro. I just don't want to travel the Hershey Highway myself." He thumbs his chest and grins. "I dig the chicks. The vagina is where it's at."

Beth's breath leaks out of her like helium from a deflating balloon.

Jeb glowers, and Maddie rolls her eyes. "Kinda homophobic, Jacky. And verbiage. Duh."

Jeb pushes away from the wall. His skintight shorts, which leave very little to the imagination, force Beth to look away, a flush rising. She's become too aware of Jeb Merrick's body.

She likes it—and she doesn't need the complication right now. He seems to sense her feelings and studies her with half-hooded eyes.

Beth looks everywhere but at him. She swears she can feel his self-satisfaction

Jacky glances between the two of them and opens his mouth.

"Shut up, Jacky," Maddie warns.

"What?" he asks indignantly. "I was—"

She whips her head in his direction. "I know. *Don't.*"

"Fine, God." He stuffs his hands underneath his armpits, and challenges them all with his presence.

"Let's make a plan," Beth says to break the uncomfortable silence and steer the conversation from body parts and sexual orientation. "We've eaten, cleansed, and had five hours of rest."

Jeb looks at all their faces, his eyes fastening on Beth's last. He nods in apparent agreement. "We will move to TCH then see what order, if any, Kennet and Calvin have restored, and join them in those efforts."

He looks at Jacky and Maddie. "This does not concern you directly. Neither of you are Reflectives, and you are foreigners here. You might want to sequester yourselves. Beth and I will reconnoiter our position and assess what's needed and by whom." Jeb plants his feet wide apart, hands crossing the flat planes of his chest.

Three seconds of heavy silence pass.

"Fuck that, Merrick," Jacky spits out in disgust. "You need all the help you can get in this crazy takeover bullshit. Count me in."

Beth holds her breath for Jeb's reply.

A smile ghosts Jeb's lips. "That's what I was afraid you'd say."

Beth releases the breath and looks at Maddie's thin body and too-long hair. "I'd like to give Maddie's hair a trim and bundle her up a little better. She's been surviving on garbage and thievery. It'd take longer to braid all that hair than to just cut some off."

"Okay," Jeb agrees slowly, surveying Maddie's condition with eyes that miss nothing. "Jacky and I will get clothing from my domicile and return here within the hour."

Beth's eyes sweep the second-skin shorts that Jeb wears.

He catches her eye and his lips quirk.

The bastard knows she was admiring the view.

They leave before she can think of anything clever to say.

Maddie says it for her. "Jeb is *hot*."

She doesn't say anything when Beth blushes beat red. That was exactly what Beth was thinking.

7

Merrick

Jeb studies Jacky with a critical eye. He is not built like a Reflective, but he is not small of stature, either.

Jeb circles the youth, noting the too-long cuffs at the sleeves of the borrowed shirt and the pants that drag the ground.

Still, he is every bit of one hundred eighty-five centimeters. *A good height, though somewhat short for a Reflective.*

Stop that, Jeb. He is not a Reflective—he never will be.

Beth is short, and she was hades on wheels as a Reflective. Jeb winces at the thought. He now loathes the idea of her fighting. He doesn't care if TC needs her.

Jeb is bonded to her. And he knows deep within his being that he could not go on without Beth.

She remains blissfully ignorant of the scope and depth of his feelings due to the bond. That knowledge fouls his mood.

"Do I pass the test?"

"Huh?" Jeb looks up. He'd stopped moving—his eyes were at his feet.

Beth undoes him. All the conventions and things of importance disappear when countered by the soul bond.

"You're fine," Jeb says.

"What is your major malfunction?" Jacky's question comes across as a goad.

Jeb reins in his temper. "I'm clearly distracted. My home world has been turned upside down. My former partner is now my soul mate—yet she doesn't ken to it. And I have two Threes I'm responsible for, and I don't know the first thing about tending them."

"Pfft! We're not pets, Merrick. We can 'tend' to ourselves. I never signed up for babysitting, and I don't think Maddie needs your charity."

Jeb's mouth parts.

"As for Jasper? She's going to just have to let that internal timepiece of hers keep on ticking until she finds out what's what. Personally, I think it's a dose of karma come to kick you in your ass."

Jeb leans forward. "Is there anything else you can divulge yourself of?"

Jacky cocks his head, tapping his chin for a handful of seconds. "Now that ya mention it—"

"Shut. Up."

Jacky's mouth closes.

"Listen here, miscreant."

Jacky's eyebrows fly up. "I know that's not a nice word."

"Ah!" Jeb yells into his domicile and stalks off. He takes several deep breaths and finally walks back to where Jacky stands.

"Papilio needs you. Maddie needs you. Do you think it would be too much trouble to just—if you would control your impulses?"

Jacky shrugs. "Sure, say the magic words." He mimes polishing his knuckles on his ill-fitting shirt.

Jeb wants to hit him. Instead he hisses, "Please."

"Nope," Jacky says, giving him a look of anticipation.

Jeb's lived a long time. He's been to Three many times. His brows collide when he hits on what Jacky might want.

"I need you."

"Bingo!" Jacky says, moving to the door. He swings it wide. "Coming?"

Jeb follows the boy, glaring at his back the entire way back to Beth's domicile.

Jeb is amazed there's any health left in the nearly black tendrils of Maddie's hair, living as she has on whatever she could find.

Beth rounds the corner, butterflies hovering around her body like a halo of color.

She has yet another full plate of food stuffs.

"Hi," she greets him, smiling.

Jeb's chest tightens.

Her face falls. "What is it?" She scans him and Jacky, obviously seeing nothing superficially amiss.

It's not superficial.

Jeb lets his hand drop from where he was rubbing his chest.

"Nothing," he answers.

Their eyes lock, and Beth slowly moves toward him. She places the tray on the table; Maddie and Jacky sit down and begin eating.

"We always eat last," Jeb murmurs, more for something to say than to convey valuable information.

Beth nods. She reaches for his hand, and he resists at first.

He wants her to choose for herself.

"No, Jeb, let me help you."

Beth slides her arms around his waist, and he sighs, feeling the painful knot loosen.

"Better?" she asks.

He nods.

Jeb has heard the rumors—he just didn't believed them.

Soul mates need to be in the presence of the other for optimal ease.

Jeb holds back a snide laugh. *Ease of who?*

Because Jeb thinks there's nothing *easy* about this mess.

He turns his head and lays it atop Beth's head, inhaling her sweet fragrance.

"How come they didn't make you right away? Didn't Ryan know you'd stayed with Beth?" Jacky asks Maddie.

Jeb admits he's curious, and gives Maddie an inquisitive look.

Beth continues walking but is silent.

"I found a trapdoor thingy."

Beth whirls. "That's how you avoided entrapment."

"Yes—they came *all* the time, at first. I could hear them…talking."

Jeb slows, turning to her. "About what?"

Maddie bites her lip and sucks back a sob. Beth squeezes her thin shoulder. "I'll tell you what I can repeat."

"Those fucktards," Jacky seethes.

"Jacky," Jeb warns.

He slaps his thighs with his palms. "Disagree with me, Merrick."

Jeb can't. "Go on, please," he encourages Maddie.

"They wanted to find me, especially Ryan. He wanted to use me first."

Jeb doesn't think she's even aware she shivers at the mention of Lance Ryan's name. His jaw clenches.

"He didn't hurt the butterflies," she offers as if it is the only good thing she experienced during the siege.

"No Reflective would harm a papilion," Jeb states.

"Oh, I don't know, Merrick." Maddie expels a shaking breath.

She tosses her thick braid behind her back, and Jeb allows a small smile. Beth wasted no time in taming the young woman's hair.

"But after the first year, they only came once a month. It's been two years since they came last."

"You must have been terrified," Beth says.

Maddie scans their faces. "I still am."

"Hey—Mad, nobody's gonna getcha now. It's you and me against the world. It's not great, but it's better than Chuck, right?"

Maddie looks at Jacky then away. "It's kinda like Chuck in a way. Always looking over my shoulder, wondering when he would find me and kick my teeth in."

Jacky laughs, startling Maddie.

Jeb wonders what the hades is so funny.

"I think Chuckie-boy is worm feast." His mossy-green eyes land on Jeb, who gives a grim nod.

"Five years now."

"Rotting?" Jacky presses with a knowing smile.

A slow grin overtakes Jeb's face. "Oh yes, positively ground sludge at this point."

Maddie laughs.

It's good to see a smile on her face, regardless of the reason.

Jeb views Jacky in a new light. He possesses no tact, but the boy is as shrewd as a fox.

He lifted the oppression from Maddie like an unseen veil. She steps forward, looping her arm through his, and they begin walking again.

Jacky looks at Jeb in profile and winks.

It's deeply troubling that Rachett has not been found. There is no effective Reflective leadership without him.

Interim leadership will fall to a vote.

Calvin and Kennet are worn and filthier than even Jeb's lackluster group had been. But they've accomplished a lot in the day and a half since their jump to Papilio.

They've scoured The Cause Headquarters. Blood and bullets have been cleaned away, and the broken butterfly sculpture has been repaired and remounted. After all, it is the metaphorical flag of their world.

Jeb's eyes cut a swath in the general vicinity of the sculpture.

The money changer is gone, and the treads of marbled cream and apricot are pure again. A little bit of blood is visible only if one looks for it.

Jeb strides to Kennet and claps him on the back. Calvin's eyes widen at the sight of Maddie. Wisely, he doesn't comment on her obvious frailty.

"Good Principle, how is it a Three survived this?"

Jeb lifts a shoulder. "It is her tale to tell, and a longer one than we have time for at present."

"True," Calvin agrees.

Strained silence tightens between them. "What—how do we assess things?" Jeb asks.

"While you were getting prettied up—" Kennet says in a mocking voice.

"I am not, and will never be, *pretty*. But I am fed, bathed, and have five hours sleep underneath my belt."

Calvin palms his chest above his heart. "Oh, the envy!"

"Report," Jeb commands dryly, softening the word with a smile.

Their faces smooth to seriousness and Jeb's heart accelerates. In his experience, no pause is a good one.

"There have been some papiliones women spared, but too few," Kennet speaks to the ground. "The Reflectives have returned to the domiciles they once had, but…" He spreads his hands away from his body.

"Many were destroyed," Calvin finishes quietly.

Hands clenched into fists, Jeb closes his eyes against the thought of their women being used in that way.

Jeb opens his eyes slowly, inhaling deeply. "Rachett?"

They shake their heads in unison.

Jeb turns to let Beth know what is happening, then he feels a pluck at his sleeve.

He turns back.

"The news is grim, my friend."

Worse than what's happened to our world for the last five years?

"Before we killed the defected Reflectives, they anticipated our coming."

Jeb leans into Calvin, their eyes meet. "And?"

"They Reflected the women."

Jeb jerks back as though burnt, his face as tight as a mask. "Where?" he whispers.

Kennet shakes his head. "Everywhere."

8

Slade

"I do not believe for one minute that Dimitri has tasked you with a Sector Ten jump for the sole purpose of reconnaissance." Gunnar nods at the young woman.

She smiles. "Thank you so much, sir."

"No. Thank you." He smiles, revealing fangs tinged pink with her blood.

Slade rolls his eyes, giving a hard sigh.

Three papiliones stand before them, staring blankly.

"Eeny, meeny, miny, moe." Gunnar tosses his finger from one to the other. "I've had you first." He gives the young woman a brief nod, and she shines a face-breaking smile upon him.

"And now I shall have—"

"Gunnar," Slade says.

"Hmm," he replies, hand palming his chin.

"Stop this. Take the blood and be done with it."

Gunnar looks at him, deep eyes regarding Slade with barely contained tolerance. "I will have my fill and fun at the same time."

The young woman shivers.

Gunnar notices, grinning wider, if possible.

"And look..." Gunnar slowly spins. "No more gaping wounds."

"Yes, and I'm sure that all will get stalled on the *wounds*." Slade's eyebrows rise. "It wouldn't possibly be your Bloodling good looks."

"Yes, well, I do make a fine specimen."

Gunnar stalks forward, grabs the next woman, and strikes her hard in the throat—for the second time.

The young woman, who shivered earlier, takes a step back. Seeing so much blood probably gives her pause.

Gunnar puts her aside and delicately wipes the blood away with the back of his hand, smearing it like the lipstick some females wear.

"You don't *seem* insane," Slade comments.

Half a day's travel is not enough time for Slade to know for certain, but Gunnar acts like any other Bloodling, with a greater appetite.

"I am not." He moves to the third woman.

Slade gives him an incredulous expression. "You haven't had your fill?"

He smirks. "No."

After he bleeds the final Papilio, he walks to a nearby tree and leans back against the trunk, one leg bent, the other planted at the base.

He parts his lips and barks a hearty belch into the still forest. "That was excellent."

He points his laser gaze at the three Papiliones women, so deep under his thrall, they probably couldn't recite their own names.

"You are dismissed."

They startle as one and begin to mill around. One bumps into the next.

"Gunnar..."

He chuckles, then his face becomes serious as he shoots Slade a hard look. "All right. You're no fun." His expression becomes speculative. "You will return to your..." He cocks his eyebrows, glancing in Slade's direction.

"Domiciles," Slade replies dryly.

"Yes—and not remember your encounter with myself." He looks to Slade again, his lips curling. "Or my colleague."

They nod, looking first at him then at Slade. They walk off, more or less in the direction of where Slade assumes their homes are located.

"That went well," Gunnar says.

"Not really."

Gunnar exhales, pushing off the trunk. He saunters over to where Slade stands. "To answer your earlier question: I am quite sane, despite my unjust incarceration."

They square off.

"I worked for your sire as captain of the Bloodling guard for three centuries, Slade. I know the tenor of my position—my mind." He taps his temple.

"You killed thirty nightlopers."

He swings to face Slade. An ebony strand of hair comes loose from its binding and falls across his face. Gunnar flicks it away. "Only the ones associated with Lucinda."

"No matter how vague the tie to her rape and murder—they all suffered by your hand. There is not a spot in our history that speaks of a greater mass murder than the one you committed. That is why you were in prison."

Gunnar moves with the speed of their vampire ancestors, and his chest is an inch from Slade's in the blink of an eye. "I was in Bloodling prison because Dimitri convinced your father that I was a threat to all beings, not just the ones responsible for Lucinda's murder."

His face seethes at mine. I see the insanity in his gaze. I also see rage, passion—and the barest bit of temperance.

"If I had been free, do you think your father would be dead? Do you think Dimitri could so easily have taken our females?"

Slade's mind reels. He had assumed all along that Gunnar was a danger to Bloodlings. All the while, Gunnar's imprisonment was the machinations of a nightloper greedy for power, taking his biggest opposition out of the way.

"Dimitri is responsible for Daven's death?" Slade asks slowly. He must be sure; it puts everything in a different light.

Gunnar nods curtly. "Yes. Though the poison was not found in your father's system and he was nearly a thousand years old, it is true."

"Once your father and I were out of his way, Dimitri moved on to the females."

"Crippling our reproduction," Slade states in terrible confirmation.

"Yes," Gunnar hisses. "That—and only that—is the reason I jumped with you. I will be regarded as a loosed felon. My risk is no more than extra jail time. But for the chance to find my own flesh and blood? Or to find the man responsible for the mercy killing of Lucinda? It is well worth it. Who knows? Maybe we can find allies willing to overthrow Dimitri, put an end to the slaving and his rule." His hand closes into a clumsy fist because his talons are too long. "Maybe we take back our females."

I'm here to take your daughter to the very man who imprisoned our race.

Gunnar's hand claps Slade's shoulder. "What troubles you?"

My deceit, Slade thinks but doesn't say.

"It is much to adjust to."

Gunnar's eyes become hooded. "Perhaps you should have sought the answers yourself, instead of bloodshed and useless scheming to procure our females."

Slade whirls on him, shaking off his hand. "There were not enough Bloodlings to fight for our females."

Gunnar nods slowly. "But with me, we could get them back."

"You're one Bloodling. *One.*" Slade bares his fangs.

He studies Slade. "This is not a numbers game, prince—but a battle of strategy. It will not be won with bloodlust, feuding and loss of life." Gunnar taps his temple. "It will be won with intellect, every bit as fine of a weapon as the one you hold at your waist."

Slade's hand reflexively moves to his weapons belt.

Gunnar nods and smiles. "I have you thinking in another direction."

"Yes." *He has no idea.*

Gunnar rubs his hands together, looking around him. "Well now, we've fed." He looks at Slade. "Or rather, *I've* fed."

He begins walking. "First order of business is to locate Commander Rachett and thank him."

Slade follows hesitantly.

"Thank him for what?"

"For killing Lucinda."

Slade halts, watching Gunnar's broad back as he continues toward the outline of buildings far in the distance. They'd been lucky to stumble across women picking berries at the edge of the forest. The majority of inhabitants were miles beyond them.

No doubt sensing Slade did not follow, Gunnar turns. "What?"

"I thought nightlopers—"

"They did," Gunnar says in a flat voice. "But her people came to save her. Ultimately, Rachett did the hardest thing. The best thing. He killed her so she might be free of the agony."

He walks back to where Slade stands. The fiery ball of the sun begins to sink behind him, backlighting Gunnar in scarlet. The stains of his feed look like cast patches of shadow over his face, hands, and neck.

"Lucinda was too injured to live. Even her extensive recuperative abilities couldn't make her whole. So Rachett ended her suffering."

He turns away, sadness etched on every plane of his face. "I came when she was gone."

"And you killed them."

He whirls, his eyes blazing at Slade. A trick of the dying sun creates bloody pools there. "Not all."

"Dimitri." Slade states as fact.

"Precisely."

Silence rules the two Bloodlings for another full minute, then Gunnar claps his hands together. "Let's go get her, shall we?"

"Who?" Slade asks, unable to hide his surprise.

"Why that hopper you've got your heart set on, who is also my daughter."

He knows. Gunnar knows I'm here to steal Beth for Dimitri.

"The tiny Reflective—I hear everything. There is no secret that is too buried for my ears."

"What did you hear?" Slade asks quietly, fearing a dagger in his back the minute it's turned.

"That you lust after her, of course."

He flips his fingers toward himself. "Moonlight is burning. Let us be on our way." Gunnar continues on without waiting for Slade's response.

That is good.

Slade couldn't have said anything even if he wanted to.

9

Beth

"A word?" Jeb interrupts Beth as she converses with other Reflectives.

Their faces swivel to Jeb then her.

Heat rises to Beth's face. So much has changed since they were here as reluctant partners. She's helpless to remove the new component to their relationship, and she's ill-equipped to navigate the unfamiliar and treacherous waters of their new relationship.

Jeb doesn't seem to have that trouble.

His tone of voice says so much, and her shoulders stiffen in anticipation of his next words.

Beth's heart had lifted at the sight of The Cause Headquarters being put to rights. *But now…now Jeb's back to the hard soldiering Reflective of before.*

Not a trace of the tender Jeb remains.

Jeb takes her gently by the elbow, and Beth tries to ignore the burning eyeballs at her back.

"Rachett is nowhere to be found," he announces quietly.

Beth nods, her spirit sinking at confirmation of terrible news, but it makes sense. Rachett was the logical Reflective to put out of commission if a takeover had been in the making.

It's what Beth would've done.

"Yes," Beth answers, keeping pace with Jeb's long strides away from the knot of Reflectives keeping tabs on their every move. "I've been made aware."

"Did you also know that the female Reflectives have been jumped?"

Beth spins to face him, her heart lodged inside her throat as she grips his arm.

"What? No!" she says loudly.

Jeb forgets where they are—and all semblance of professionalism—as he cups her face.

"You are all who remains."

Beth takes a shaky step away and slaps a palm into his chest. "Where are they, Jeb? Tell me!"

She's furious. "They had *no* right. The women don't have locators. Some have never jumped—not once. They're naked of protection." Beth's panic rises like bile. "We must go! Find them." Beth's voice breaks. "This is worse than their forced abuse. This is…certain death," she finishes bleakly.

Jeb grabs her hands. "I'm sorry, Beth."

She lets him pull her to his chest. Beth knows she's being weak. His soul declaration gives her the power to exploit him. But Beth finally admits, if only to herself, that she needs his strength.

She draws from Jeb like an old-fashioned battery from Three. Beth takes a sucking inhale, calming herself.

He strokes her hair. "I did not want you to find out from someone else."

She nods. "I'm sorry, Jeb. It was wrong of me to strike you."

"I'll live." His voice is dry.

Beth tips her head up, and his lips curl as his hand cups her chin.

His eyes flick over her shoulder and turn the flat gray they become when his mood darkens.

Beth slowly turns to face where his gaze lingers, and hostile eyes meet hers. She steps out of the circle of Jeb's arms.

"What's wrong?" Beth asks quietly, and he stays her with a hand.

"Think it through."

Beth doesn't want to think it through. But Jeb would've told her if he could.

She scans the sea of male Reflectives. Some faces meet hers with expressions of neutrality, but not all do.

Some expressions cause her to retreat a step. Beth does not embrace fear easily. It's not in her nature to do so.

But the numbers of hostile expressions aren't looking good.

It takes seconds for Beth to do as Jeb asked.

I'm the only female Reflective on Papilio.

And the number of males stands at greater than one hundred. The ratio blows, as Jacky would say.

"We don't like the way you behave with Reflective Jasper," a Reflective from the very back of the growing crowd comments. And the Reflectives' collective hostility transfers neatly to Jeb.

Beth takes another step backward and bumps into Jeb, whose hands fall on her shoulders.

"How I behave with Reflective Jasper doesn't concern you, Reflective Conan."

Mutterings erupt from the crowd.

Beth's heart begins to speed. "Oh my Principle—what, Jeb?"

"Yes?" he asks quietly.

I'm afraid. "What does this mean?"

He squeezes her shoulders. "Nothing good."

"What should I do?" Beth instantly scans for reflections. Many twinkle back at her. But in her home world, she'll simply be followed by any Reflectives who choose to pursue her.

Sweat breaks out on her forehead, and her mouth goes dry.

"Would you become that which we killed?" Jeb's voice rings out like a struck bell, and Beth flinches.

The whispering ceases, and Beth can't help the sick tension that creeps underneath her skin like insects invading her body.

Be strong.

Beth thinks of the Tenth: *Reconcile emotion for The Cause, not another.*

That includes herself. Beth straightens her spine. No being alive can jump better than she can.

This horrible circumstance will not end her—or define her.

Her chin kicks up a notch, and she stares the males down defiantly. She feels her Bloodling heritage sing in her veins, searing like liquid heat. Her stay in One awoke something primitive inside her, and Beth will use whatever advantage it's given her to survive.

"No, we would never hurt our females!" calls out another whom Beth doesn't know, and she allows a silent breath to ease out of her.

"Then I have no problem with saying what I must," Jeb says as he inches in front of her protectively.

Beth's heart goes from a trot to a gallop. *No, Jeb—don't tell them*. But as she thinks it, she knows he will.

"I declare Beth Jasper my soul mate. She is my other half." He raises his hand, bringing it into a tight fist, and lays it over his heart.

Beth hangs her head. *This cannot end well.*

"Impossible!" another male shouts.

"She is of mixed heritage," Jeb recites calmly. However, Beth is attuned to Jeb now, and she hears the thread of tension in his words.

"She's a mongrel—I say we end her now!"

Beth cringes at the old insult, even as she gears up to jump.

"If any think to touch a hair on her head, they can seek their end, sooner rather than later—by my hand."

"No, Jeb." Beth grabs his arm. "Don't you dare die to defend me." The warmth continues to flow, swarming her insides and radiating out to light up her fingertips and toes.

Beth sways with the sensation, feeling heavy and light simultaneously, as though she is laden debris and moving swiftly in a river whose waters run warm.

Jeb whirls, grabbing her shoulders. His eyes are deep pewter—flat and angry. "There's *no* choice, Beth. None. I'm bound to you, body and soul. The precepts of soul bonding is a great theory we've been taught. I'm here to tell you the bond is unfathomable in reality."

Tears spring to Beth's eyes, and she fights gravity to keep them there. This great Reflective has been brought low by her existence.

I can save him from himself.

If she were not in Papilio, Jeb would have nothing to protect. Her eyes restlessly search out every reflective surface. Lightposts shimmer back at her; puddles, sunglasses, even windows taunt her with their potential.

A Reflective male moves forward, and his blade glints in the sun.

Heat builds within her.

"Beth—no!" Jeb must certainly sense her readiness to jump.

So do some of the Reflectives nearby. They move as a unit, running toward Jeb and Beth.

She flings her gaze around her, gauging both difficulty for others to follow her jump and proximity to her location.

Wide, frantic eyes land on her and Jeb.

"I'm sorry—it's for the best. Protect Maddie," Beth tells him in a low voice.

Jeb's grip tightens.

"No, Beth," he says, ignoring the siege of Reflectives storming toward them. "This isn't the way."

A torch lights within Beth, igniting a pathway.

Jeb's eyes flick to above her shoulder and widen with shock…and something else.

Beth decides it's fear before a second hand grabs her free arm and a Bloodling male stares down into her face.

Time grinds to a surreal halt. Beth instantly knows who he is.

"Father?" she says, as both question and answer.

Eyes so like her own move to Jeb and dismiss him immediately. Then Beth sees *him*—a man who looks Papiliones, but isn't.

She would know Slade anywhere.

"What…" Beth starts to ask, beginning to jerk her arm away, and then she's jumping.

The one reflective surface she dismissed as too difficult even for her skill level is what her newfound father uses: the fountain spray in the court pavilion before the TCH steps.

A tall bronze sculpture rises from a deep pool of water. The figure of a Reflective male takes center stage, fingertips reaching for the elusive butterfly just out of reach as his hand holds a bowl of water meant to entice the butterfly. Water sprouts from his parted lips, dumping into the bowl, then spraying into the large pool at his feet.

Heat caresses her skin, then she slams into the microscopic spray with a finesse she's never felt.

Her scream echoes in the pathway her biological father creates.

But her terror doesn't move him—Beth fears nothing will.

10

Slade

Slade forgot how beautiful Beth Jasper really is. Certainly, the old Three saying "absence makes the heart grow fonder" could apply, but Slade thinks it might just be good old-fashioned lust he's feeling.

Or worse, he might actually care for the hopper.

Gunnar throws them out of the waterfall and directly into the ruins of one of the Papilio quadrants.

Beth lands smoothly, as if her guts have no qualms about the flight they just took.

On the other hand, Slade does all he can to keep his breakfast in his belly. He belches softly behind his fist and smells vomit.

"Rough landing?" Gunnar asks with a bone-rattling clap on Slade's back. He hisses from the abrupt contact, forgets he doesn't have fangs, and punches Gunnar straight in the face.

The older Bloodling staggers backward and grins. He coldcocks Slade right in his roiling guts, knocking him hard on his rump.

Slade grunts, holding his stomach, and slits his eyes at Beth, hating how the jump has compromised him.

She's crouched, dark eyes flashing. "Slade?" she asks in a low voice.

He nods, feels a second wash of vertigo, and stops all movement.

"Why do you look Reflective?" Her eyes remain on Gunnar, who turns his full attention to her.

"Clever of you to extradite yourself during the jump," he comments blandly.

Beth rolls her shoulders, straightening. "It's rudimentary training for Reflectives. A good Reflective can move during a jump."

"Disguise," Slade croaks, finally answering her question.

Beth tilts her head, assessing Slade. "Not a very good one."

Slade snorts, getting to his hands and knees. He pushes off to a standing position and manages not to sway.

"Good enough." He groans and swallows quickly to ward off spilling the contents of his stomach.

He hates the show of weakness, especially since Beth and Gunnar are completely unaffected.

Chuckling, Gunnar cocks an eyebrow. "You have your mother's heart." He takes a step toward Beth, and a naked ceramic blade is suddenly in her overhanded grip. She waves it back and forth. "Stay as you are, Bloodling."

Gunnar spreads his palms inoffensively away from his body. "This is not the reunion I would have anticipated." A smile ghosts his lips.

Beth dismisses her father's attempt at humor. "I didn't know until three seconds ago that you existed."

Gunnar's lips turn up in a sideways smile of contemplation. "Ah yes, I see. Immaculate conception."

"Hmm, a comedian. Wonderful." Beth tosses a look Slade's way. However, he can't respond; he's busy holding up a tree trunk.

"Slade, is he—why are *you* here?"

For you. "Reconnaissance."

Beth splits her gaze between Slade and Gunnar. "Bullshit."

It's only a moment's diversion, and Gunnar is suddenly there in front of her.

What did he reflect with—or is he just that *fast?*

She moves into his charge, bringing the hilt of the ceramic blade underneath his chin with jaw-dropping hardness.

Gunnar drops, and as he falls, he grabs her wrist, yanking her down on top of him.

Beth releases the blade and slaps his face. His flesh rings in the deadness of their surroundings.

She leaps into a somersault and rolls away from him then springs to a stand.

He's instantly in front of her, fangs bared. "I mean you no harm!" he roars into her face.

Slade's lips curl. Gunnar *looks* as though he means a great deal of harm.

"Then back the fuck off, Bloodling!" she shouts back.

Gunnar steps away, working his jaw back and forth with his large hand.

Slade grins. *Tiny frog.*

"Thanks for the help, Slade," Beth shoots his way.

He shrugs. "He won't hurt you—he is your sire." No Bloodling would ever hurt his female kin. It is not done.

"Pfft. The manhandling is a deal breaker."

"Three slang," Gunnar says with a slight sneer as mild irritation finally begins to bleed through his jovial exterior.

Beth frowns, keeping a close eye on him. "What of it? It *is* my job, you know—to jump."

Gunnar smiles, pacing a circle around her. "And what else is your job?"

She turns with his movements as she answers automatically, "To uphold The Cause."

"Your mother held the Thirteenth in the highest regard."

Beth swallows hard, and Slade feels a wave of pity for her that is so strong, it staggers him.

"Forsake not The Cause," she recites softly.

"Yes," Gunnar hisses in obvious resentment.

Beth's curiosity is an ill-fitting mask that covers all other emotions. Yet she stays the course. Slade's admiration for her swells. Beth has the heart of a lioness nightloper.

Her chin rises. "In the end, it is all we have."

Gunnar waves away her words. "Yes, yes, *yes*. The precious *Cause*—the murderer of your mother."

Beth pales, and the hand holding the blade, which she snatched off the ground, trembles ever so slightly.

"Murdered?" she whispers. "By you?"

Gunnar throws back his head and howls into the sky.

Beth drops the weapon to cover her ears. The call of a Bloodling is a beautiful thing, and it restores Slade at the primal level. For a partial-blood like Beth, with her acute Reflective hearing, it would be a discordant scream.

Gunnar strides to Beth, and she backs away, hands still over her ears, forgetting her weapon in the trampled grass.

He jerks her hands from her ears and holds them against her sides.

Beth doesn't struggle.

Nothing in the known thirteen sectors is stronger than a Bloodling. They're nearly unstoppable.

Slade does not believe Beth's aware of the tears that trace down a face so filled with loss, the scene etches his mind as her grief unfolds before him.

"No," Gunnar says in a tight voice of raw agony, "I loved her—with the blood that pumps within my veins, with the thoughts of my mind, with each breath that entered and left my body. I loved her."

His fangs gleam as he hisses his anguish.

The Bloodling towers over his small Reflective daughter, but they are somehow a match, their genetics more alike than not.

"Then who killed her?" Beth's tears soak her Reflective uniform. "Who. Killed. My. Mother? If not you, then who?"

Slade sees thoughts of vengeance wash over her face like water sheeting off glass.

"So many, my little hopper." He thumbs away her tears, and Beth shivers. "But ultimately, it was your own Commander Rachett who ended my Lucinda."

"No!" Beth backs away, hands covering her mouth, shock widening her eyes.

Gunnar holds up a palm, stalking her. "It was mercy, not murder. Lucinda was too damaged to heal herself."

Surprise momentarily blanks her face. "Who?" Beth repeats.

His hand falls. "Nightlopers."

Extreme emotions do battle across her features as seconds transform into a full minute. Slade watches her regain hard-won composure. "Why didn't *you* come for me?"

"Come?" Gunnar's eyebrows hike.

"Yes!" Beth says, spinning, her laughter holding a slight edge of hysteria. "I was a pariah as a Reflective. They had a whole jeering section for Beth Jasper. Female—*mongrel*."

Gunnar flinches at her wounded tone, grabbing her with his massive hands. "You are no mongrel. You are the daughter of a union between Reflective and Bloodling warriors. That is supremacy, not inferiority."

Beth's struggles with her painful emotions, moving out from underneath Gunnar's hands.

"I was unaware of your existence," Gunnar explains.

Beth whirls, facing him. "What? Why?"

"I do not know. Your mother would have her reasons to keep the knowledge of a daughter from me."

"We do not leave our offspring," Slade interjects, walking slowly toward Beth as though she's a skittish colt ready to run.

"You did." Her nearly black eyes pin Gunnar with accusation, but he shakes his head in the face of it.

"No," he replies softly. "I did not. Your mother understood full well that if I had known I had offspring—especially with her—I would jump here and take you away from this life of hardship."

A sigh full of longing seeps out of Beth. "Why would she keep me a secret? What could be gained from that? Why would she not claim me herself?" Beth bites her lip to stop its quaking.

A sad uplift touches Gunnar's mouth. "My speculation is she sought to protect you."

"From what?" Beth's brows pinch together.

"From whom?" Gunnar looks at Slade, and he clamps down on his expression. Slade believes he knows exactly why Lucinda chose to keep her pregnancy secret. She could have easily hidden the birth if she was willing to compromise the Twelfth.

Slade excavates his memory and finally remembers the second-to-last directive: *Disturb not the Continuum.*

Yes, it would be possible for Lucinda to go through an entire pregnancy and give birth in any sector other than Ten or One, and no one would have been the wiser, even Gunnar.

"Who raised you?" Slade asks suddenly.

"Adoptive parents." Beth's voice is full of unresolved shock.

"The life of a female Reflective is wrought with conflict, and proving yourself constantly," Gunnar says.

"No shit," Beth comments with an uneasy laugh.

Gunnar frowns. "Your mother said her life within The Cause was not an easy one."

"It would have been worse than anything I went through—she was even earlier than I was." Beth tugs at the end of her braid, working her finger through the tail. "My mother," she adds softly as though speaking it aloud might conjure her.

He nods solemnly. "She must have seen your role as a female Reflective warrior as the lesser of the two evils."

Beth smiles, then begins to laugh. She brays like a donkey, slapping her thighs and whooping as tears stream down her face.

Slade and Gunnar glance at each other, frowning in unison.

"Yup! That whole Reflective *beat down* was a barrel of fucking monkeys to live through." Beth slaps her chest with her hand. "But now it's what I am." She bares her teeth at them. "*I am Reflective.* I was born to be. I just wish to Principle that even one person had been in my corner. And principledamned Rachett knew all along. *All along.*" Beth's voice begins to warm with her rage.

"And how in hades did I know who you were?" Her eyes leap from Slade's to Gunnar's.

"You are my kin—the fire is proof of that, though it fades after time and proximity."

Gunnar touches his finger lightly to his own chest.

Beth follows, laying her palm across her own.

"Now what?" she asks, tossing her braid behind her and putting hands to hips.

"Why now, we may return to One, of course" Gunnar says with a self-assured smile.

Slade tenses. Somehow, he doesn't think this is how Dimitri sees things happening.

Beth's brows knot, and her mouth opens and closes. Her lips part again. "Uh—no. I'm not going anywhere," she replies slowly, as though Gunnar is a somewhat dim-witted child, and throws out her palms. "The Cause *must* be restored. I have unfinished business—Threes who need me, and Jeb—" Beth bites her lip, and Slade is instantly on alert at the mention of the Reflective male's name. He reads her face and scents her emotions. He knows the taste of her blood.

Even now, the remnants pound through his veins.

Slade senses Reflective Merrick thinks to claim Beth.

Over my dead blood.

Beth lifts her face to Gunnar, hands flying to settle on her hips again in clear dismissal. “I am Reflective. I will not be remanded to One. It’s not where I belong.”

Gunnar steps forward, never breaking eye contact with Beth. “It is the only place you shall ever belong.”

11

Merrick

"Beth!" Jeb roars, spinning slowly in a circle. Each raw pulse point of his body feels like small incinerating spots of scorching heat.

Voices explode all around him.

"What the hades was that?"

"Did you see that? Was that male a One?"

"Bloodling, for sure—"

Jeb stops spinning. He scans for Beth with his eyes, and finally lets his mind do it instead.

He reaches far and wide, spreading out feelers as antiquated as time to find his soul mate.

Jeb ignores his twisting insides. Beth is out of sight, and he was finally doing so well emotionally. He didn't go insane when she insisted on putting herself in danger, he gave her space, and he was courteous when his every nerve ending was on fire to make her his—claim her.

Now she's gone. A Bloodling and a Reflective companion who felt all wrong have jumped with his soul mate.

The tailwind is the finest ribbon, already dissipated as he stands in a shell-shocked stupor.

Jeb plows through the mob of Reflectives, who moments ago, thought they would control Beth.

It should be funny really, though Jeb can't see the humor.

Before, they wouldn't have deigned to think of her as Reflective. But when Reflective women are scarce, even a half-breed like Beth holds appeal.

But she is mine.

Jeb clips the shoulder of a Reflective on his mad dash to the fountain. "Hey!"

Jeb shoves him aside, sprinting for the trail still lingering beside the fountain.

He reaches forward, scooping the glittering remnants, and brings them toward his face.

He wafts his palm backward and forward.

Got it.

Jeb can't jump the same trail, but he knows where it goes. He turns his gaze on the throng, his brows sinking.

"Silence!" he bellows.

The crowd of male Reflectives quiet. "I'm ashamed at the majority of you."

Sullen and watchful, he takes them in. Jeb's got his work cut out for him. Five years is a hades span of time for the lot of them to be unmanned.

"Beth Jasper is a fellow warrior of The Cause—not a bone to be fought over. You know what she is to me. What that means."

Eyes cast themselves to the ground. But one gaze meets his in challenge.

Jeb's hands fist. *I don't have time for a battle when Beth is missing.*

"And your supposed soul mate is with a Bloodling? That does not bode well," Reflective Conan challenges.

"No. That is why I must pursue her, immediately."

"And what of the Reflective male?" Conan presses.

Jeb shakes his head. "Do you know him?"

Jeb doesn't know every Reflective, but he considers himself familiar with all their faces after so much time together.

That Reflective was unknown to Jeb.

Verbal measles break out, and Jeb leaves the group like the disease it's become. He hikes toward a streetlamp, praying to Principle that the reflection portals still work on command.

"Wait!" Calvin rushes to catch up with him.

Jeb keeps striding, his eyes focused on the tall lamp just ahead. "Not now, Calvin."

Calvin grabs his arm, spinning Jeb around, and it's all he can do not to strike him.

"Let me come with you."

Jeb thinks of Jacky and Maddie.

His eyes sweep over the crowd. He doesn't see them.

"Where are the Threes?" Jeb asks tersely.

"With Kennet."

Jeb's shoulders drop. At least that much is in order.

"Fine, but they"—Jeb points to the group of Reflectives—"need to stop worrying about the one female that is mine and start strategizing a way to reacquire our women who've been scattered to the sectors."

Calvin's eyes level on Jeb, and he nods. "Agreed."

Their gazes shift to the hidden pocket where the portal is.

"You don't still have your device?" Calvin asks.

Jeb shakes his head. He misplaced his pulse device while on One.

"We'll use mine." Calvin brushes his thumb over the dock pad, and the hidden pocket alongside the streetlamp housing opens like a reluctant eyelid.

A mirror winks at them.

Jeb gives a covert eye flick to the crowd of Reflectives still arguing behind him.

With a disgusted shake of his head, he concentrates on the small square piece of glass.

He sees his eye blink back at him—and jumps.

His destination is the burned out quadrant of Adlaine. Beth's home quadrant.

Jeb jogs in a large circle upon his final jump. He moved through only eight portals before landing in Adlaine.

Even his usual lack of sympathy for the dregs of Papilio is plucked with what fills his vision.

The tavern where he was treated so abysmally is completely gone. A few sorrowful bricks serve as testimony to a chimney that warmed the bar in the cooler months. Damp soot clings to every surface like ashy tears mourning the devastated architecture

Jeb sighs.

Calvin bumps into him. “Sorry.”

“Klutz,” Jeb says without heat.

Calvin smirks. “You sound so Three.”

Jeb shrugs, beginning his perusal of the immediate environment.

Beth is not here.

His eyes track footprints—fresh ones.

“Look here,” Calvin says. The light reflecting off the charred buildings dulls his platinum hair.

“I see.”

Calvin is pointing to an obvious post-jump landing. Two sets of footprints are proof of a smoothly executed jump.

The other set show a staggering dump off.

Calvin says, “Looks like one of them took three steps then collapsed.”

Jeb walks to the mess of footprints and sinks to his haunches. He traces a fingertip through the revolution of misplaced gait then an obvious full-body imprint.

Calvin closes his eyes and tips his head back. “I smell—vomit.”

Jeb smiles grimly. "*Someone's* not a jumper. The male is not Reflective."

"He sure looked the part."

Jeb nods. He had—but not. "Superficially. But remember, even that prick Conan said he'd never laid eyes on him before."

"Merrick, you know we don't know the entire command. Beth stood out as female. But the rest of the men blend, especially the inductees."

His comment makes Jeb think of Lance Ryan, who is still unaccounted for.

Marvelous.

"But you didn't know him?"

Calvin shrugs. "No."

"He would handle a jump better than a drunk swagger and vomit session." Jeb's palm sweeps the remnants on the mashed grass.

Calvin frowns, scrubbing the blond stubble at his chin. "Yes," he admits slowly.

"So we are dealing with a Bloodling who took Beth for reasons unknown."

Calvin's eyebrow rises. "Or known."

Jeb glowers.

"Merrick, you have to consider the possibility that it's a blood reprisal or some such bullshit. Beth was on One long enough to make enemies."

"Fine. Perhaps. But the other male? He is no Reflective. So why would they go to all this trouble for a female from Ten? It's suicide to come in here for one female."

Calvin shakes his head. "It sure would be if everything was as it was before. When Rachett was overseer. When the Reflectives worked for The Cause and only that. Now, with the turmoil and dissension, it's a perfect time for Ones to come in and stir the pot. Those who can jump."

Jeb's restless feet take him around the perimeter of the main set of footprints. They grow wide then suddenly disappear.

"She wouldn't go with them voluntarily."

"I wouldn't think so," Calvin agrees.

Jeb gives him a sharp look.

"Merrick, she's your soul mate, but her timepiece is not degraded. As far as she's concerned, you're a player—arrogant but trustworthy. She doesn't look at you the way you look at her."

"Principle!" Jeb yells. "This is so damned frustrating!"

Calvin exhales roughly. "Let's find her, Jeb."

Jeb knows where she is.

His eyes seek what he needs.

A decorative fountain, once the focal point of this quadrant sits nearly dry.

Jeb sees a reflection.

He claps Calvin on the back, gesturing toward the fountain.

He watches Calvin study the quarter meter of murky water.

"Living dangerously, Merrick."

Jeb grins for the first time today. "Always."

They jump.

The small surface doesn't reflect well, but Jeb slams them through, using his determination and the home world advantage in his favor.

Their travel is short.

Beth's domicile is not far enough for the jump to last more than a few seconds.

12

Beth

Now that the initial shock of meeting her father has leveled off, Beth's hunger comes to life.

She's also so tired she can hardly stay standing.

Gunnar doesn't seem likely to kill her, and she knows Slade won't. With the immediate threats of physical danger gone, thoughts of Jeb crowd out Beth's other concerns. He should know she's not in imminent danger. Though all Ones are considered enemies by rote, Gunnar seems to be an exception, if a little maniacal and strange.

Beth can't stop staring. He's a massive male. Gunnar is as big as Slade and so scary to look at if she wasn't certain he meant her no harm, she would constantly be on guard.

Beth still feels edgy despite what he calls "kinship recognition," an antiquated reference Beth has read in The Cause historical volumes as a term hailing from Three, the world of spheres. It's an expression used to describe the odd surge of heat felt within when two or more people are related and in close proximity.

Beth asked Gunnar to keep his distance. She can't think with the big Bloodling looming over her. He watches her as much as she studies him.

Beth thinks her re-hydrator is completely out of food stores now. Between the two Bloodlings, they've eaten the remainder of the food.

"You eat quite a bit for a small hopper," Gunnar comments from across her domicile. He has his pointer and thumb digits close together, an obvious jab at her size.

Beth leans against the couch, crossing her feet at the ankles.

"Kicking your ass gave me an appetite." Beth's lips peel back off her teeth.

Gunnar grins, regarding her. He tosses his blade by the hilt, expertly catching it on the downward rotation, like a juggler of weapons.

She has so many questions. They crowd, polluting her mind of sane and rational thinking. He's her father, and that is mind-blowing. But he is also a dangerous Bloodling who she doesn't know. The two sides don't reconcile themselves easily.

Beth blinks, her belly full. Her heavy-lidded gaze rotates to Slade, taking in his phony Reflection façade.

"You got the eyes wrong," Beth says, swinging a finger in his direction.

Slade lids dip over eyes so dark a gray they could never fall within Reflective norms. He's still masquerading as a Reflective, which is hilarious. His appearance is more like a Reflective costume than a proper likeness. He frowns.

Beth yawns, and Gunnar's eyebrow hikes at her show of fatigue.

"Stay where you are, *Dad*," she says sarcastically as her gaze moves from Slade.

Gunnar seemed farther away the last time she looked.

Beth hiccups and slaps a hand over her mouth. Then she giggles. *What the hades is wrong with me?*

"You're too big, too," she levels her gaze on Slade.

His eyes move to black.

"Your costume is slipping," Beth says, giggling again. Her vision triples.

Beth jerks upright. Slade is suddenly beside her on the couch. Her fingers move to jab him in throat, a classic close-quarters defensive move.

He easily captures her sluggish strike and puts an arm around her shoulders. "Careful, tiny frog, don't bite the hand that feeds you."

Beth struggles to open her eyes. "Didn't feed me—I fed you." She can't stop her head from lulling onto Slade's broad shoulder.

She blinks open her eyes, feeling as if she needs toothpicks to keep them open.

Butterflies swarm above her as though warning Beth.

Gunnar moves close, and Beth mewls thickly, her body seizing into a paralytic state. "Stop—what…" Beth licks her lips. "What did you do to my food?"

Gunnar smiles. "Nothing to your food, Beth."

Sampson swirls down, and it appears Gunnar might hurt her treasured companion.

Beth grabs the only part of him she can reach—his weapons belt—and yanks the tether.

His pants fall with it. When Gunnar moves to scoop up his fallen article of clothing, Beth surges forward.

No one hurts papiliones.

With one hand on his pants, Gunnar catches Beth as she pitches forward.

Slade does too.

Jeb appears in front of her like a mirage.

Beth only has time to register his eyes moving over two Bloodlings, one with his pants at his ankles, both with their hands on her.

"Jeb—" Beth says with weak surprise then begins to crumple between the Bloodlings.

His roar follows her down into the darkness of unconsciousness.

Jeb

Jeb jogs out of the jump and into the unkempt front grounds of Beth's domicile.

Calvin lands behind him, smoothly averting a collision then circles back around to where Jeb stands.

"Positioning," Jeb announces with quiet menace.

Calvin nods, moving to Jeb's left. They creep toward her front door, where Jeb notes its lock.

Jeb plucks a duplicate key Beth gave him when they left that morning in case they were separated.

Only her unique thumbprint will work at the pulse security dock, so he must use a physical device.

Jeb remembers his uncharitable thoughts of how inane that was. When would he allow himself to not stand as protector over Beth?

His lips flatten as he pulls his ceramic switchblade.

The weapon is strictly forbidden on Ten, but Jeb acquired the black-market blade on Three.

Jeb stands at the door, placing his palm flat against the smooth, ancient wood, and regulates his breathing. He forces his mind blank and sends out that instinctive search mechanism all Reflectives have for their soul mates. He never thought he would need to employ it on his own sector, or to find a fellow Reflective.

The tendrils of clinging energy weave away from his torso, lacy vines of heat seeking Beth.

When he finds her, those appendages sing back to him.

His eyes pop open, and Calvin marvels at him. "It's true then? The soul mate legends."

Jeb nods. "So terribly true."

"But Beth Jasper." Calvin shakes his head.

Jeb wastes an unhappy look on his friend and fellow Reflective.

"Okay." Calvin swings his palms up inoffensively. "Apologies."

Jeb clenches his jaw and passes through the door, palming the flat pulse key inside his uniform pocket. They take the stairs, with Jeb gliding along the ornate handrail, Calvin opposite him.

When they reach the door marked 2, Jeb gives the barest nod to Calvin.

Jeb keeps his weapon by his side, blade out, and moves inside directly after Calvin smashes open the door with a well-placed strike of his foot.

The scene before Jeb bottoms out his stomach, nearly making him drop his weapon.

The large male Bloodling and the rogue Reflective, whom Jeb has become increasingly certain is also a Bloodling, are holding Beth between them.

The older male's lack of pants has Jeb moving before his next breath.

"Jeb," Beth says in a voice that's little more than a whisper on the air. Her soft plea incites every male instinct he possesses.

Jeb leaps from where he stands; the Bloodlings' eyes widen like slick pools of water and malice.

The older of the two drops Beth on the couch and crouches, hissing at Jeb as he barrels into him.

They roll, tumbling over the back of the couch, and slam into the half-meter solid-stone wall. Jeb leaps to a stand, and the Bloodling thumps the flats of his palms into Jeb's chest. Jeb grabs onto the tight black hair club secured at the Bloodling's nape before he flies backward.

They fall together, and Jeb releases his hold, jabbing the Bloodling in the throat. He gives a return strike to Jeb's temple, and Jeb's vision trembles.

Jeb flings himself backward, casting his arms wide, and does a backflip that takes him just out of reach of the huge Bloodling.

They circle each other, though the Bloodling's pants at his ankles causes him to shuffle.

Jeb tries to tamp down his rage at the inference of the Bloodling not having pants.

Impossible.

Jeb tenses and moves in hard, peppering his jabs at the organs protected behind bone.

Talons punch his shoulder, and Jeb grunts.

His eyes flick to Beth lying on the couch, and his adrenaline surges, ripping through to his basest level.

With a howl, he jerks his chest away, and the talons pull out of his flesh. Jeb ignores the blood—and everything but the death of this Bloodling who would harm his soul mate.

"Jeb!" Calvin shouts in the background.

The Bloodling invites him to finish him by living.

Jeb moves forward, twisting the blade he managed to hang onto into an upward arc. He sinks it deep into the Bloodling's gut. He hisses, burying his fangs in the torn meat of Jeb's shoulder.

"Stop, Reflective," the Bloodling pants beside him. "I do not wish to end you."

Jeb bares his teeth. "Fuck you."

He turns the blade, trying for the Bloodling's heart.

A hard shove loosens his hold.

Calvin comes at him, using both hands to shove him harder. "Stop! Merrick!"

Jeb turns his blade toward Calvin, his eyes flicking to Beth.

"Kill me if you want, Merrick—but it won't help Beth."

His hands grip Jeb's uniform as blood pours out of the wound. Jeb's arm whips out, hitting the wall. A wave of vertigo latches onto his vision.

"That's it, Merrick. Calm down. Beth's okay."

His eyes meet the pale blue of Calvin's. His gaze finds the strange-looking Reflective standing beside Beth then moves to the one he stabbed.

His noises of dying are satisfying to Jeb, whose smile is grim. At least he incapacitated the male before he could hurt Beth.

Then Jeb notices fire in his shoulder. He moves from underneath Calvin's hands, covering the wound on his shoulder with a slightly shaking hand.

Jeb looks to the male beside Beth. "Who are you?" Without waiting for an answer, he turns to Calvin. "Why did you stop me from finishing this one?" Jeb jerks his jaw in the direction of the struggling Bloodling at his feet.

"You'd be dead if it weren't for Beth," the second Bloodling says.

Jeb frowns. "How is that—Bloodling?"

He nods. "I am the Bloodling that fought with Ryan. I am Slade."

Jeb leans against the wall, taking in that bit of information. His eyes rake the male as the poorly rendered Reflective second skin falls away to reveal the very Bloodling who had carried away a beaten Beth.

"How does Beth have anything to do with my death?" Jeb straightens and winces at the excruciating pain in his shoulder. He pulls more healing power to the wound, redoubling his effort to close it.

Keeping a wide berth, Jeb skirts the writhing Bloodling and moves toward Beth.

"Not so fast, Reflective."

"I have soul mate claim on Beth Jasper," he says in a flat voice.

"No doubt, from your defense of her. But I think that won't matter a shit through a goose if you let her father die, do you?"

Jeb's head whips to the dying Bloodling then back to Calvin, who raises his hand slowly. "I got in there when I could, Merrick. You were going to rip that male's prick off."

He was. He still wants to.

Jeb inhales deeply, and his lungs feel bathed in fire. "So what's to stop me from finishing the job?"

Slade's flat-black irises blink back at Jeb, unnerving him. "Because she might take exception to you killing her father."

Jeb staggers back a step, his gaze riveted to the Bloodling bleeding out on Beth's stone floor.

They don't look alike.

Jeb stares.

He's wrong. They look so much alike. If he took away the Boodling's gender, size disparity and the ashy skin, they could be twins.

Slade smiles, folding his massive arms. "Now you're in a little predicament, hopper. Beth believed she was an orphan until a half hour ago. Now you will make it a reality. Claim her all you wish. I do not think Beth Jasper is a forgiving female."

He doesn't know the half of it. Beth is many-layered. If Jeb inadvertently kills her father, she might forgive him the mistake.

But would she ever forget?

13

Slade

Slade could not be more pleased. He's put Jeb Merrick soundly in his place.

The only portion spoiling the entire event is that a great warrior might die. Then Beth would be truly alone—except for himself, of course.

If Dimitri thought Slade would hand her over to him for a mate, his mind was well and truly gone.

No. Beth Jasper is *his*. She is the tiny frog meant only for him. And by exquisite coincidence, he might have removed two who would have stood as obstacles.

Slade flexes his hands, relishing having shed the tight Reflective "suit." However, now that the magic that made the covering is gone, it simply means Slade must return to One. Appearing in front of the entire command of Reflectives as one of them with the renegade Gunnar at his side wasn't so risky. That might have looked as though he had imprisoned a One. After all, what Bloodling would be foolish enough to jump to Ten with only the two of them? But if he and Gunnar were both "out" as Bloodlings in the volatile world, they would face a hundred or more Reflective warriors.

In fact, it is only a matter of time before the collective Reflectives jump to this very spot. Slade estimates they have a small window before the freed Reflectives follow Jeb Merrick's tailwind.

Right now, the love-struck fool is full of Bloodling poison and knowledge of his misdeeds. The circumstance is really too perfect.

Slade's internal musings are shattered when everything goes to hades in a handbasket and aliens move through Beth's door.

Beth

Her eyes flutter open.

Jeb.

That was the last thing she saw: Jeb charging to kill her Bloodling father.

Beth sits up, the world sways, and she falls back against the couch.

"Beth," Slade says, startling her. He's back to looking as he should—like the hardened Bloodling prince she recalls from One.

Beth ignores him, searching the room for Jeb.

Her father and Slade drugged her somehow, and she's not willing to forgive that.

She finds him. "Jeb," she calls out, but he doesn't listen, heading straight for her father.

"No—don't kill him!" Beth yells, trying to scramble off the couch.

Slade holds her.

She narrows her eyes at him. "Take your hands off me."

Slade smiles, releasing her. "Whatever you wish, tiny frog."

Beth knows nothing's ever been about what she wants and stands. The room tilts, and she stumbles forward until her hands hit the armrest of the couch.

Jeb is on his knees beside Gunnar.

The hilt of Jeb's blade is embedded in the Bloodling's chest.

"Oh, Principle," Beth says, covering her mouth.

Gunnar's arm swings up to cup her face. "My hopper."

"Jeb, do something," Beth says, putting her own hand over his. All thoughts of anger vanish in the face of his impending death.

He looks into her eyes. "I'm afraid I already did—I didn't intend to kill your father, but he stood above you, not wearing pants…I didn't know who he was, the circumstance."

A hot tear brims, then follows the line of Gunnar's cool palm as it travels down her face.

Voices boom behind them, and Beth looks around as her father's hand slips away.

Jacky and Maddie burst through the door, Reflective Kennet at their heels.

His frantic eyes take in the scene. "Thank Principle. What in hades is going on here, Jeb?"

Jeb sighs. "The Bloodlings—I thought they were harming Beth, and it turns out the opposite was true."

Beth looks up at Slade, who is stoic, adding nothing. "Slade—please, what can be done?"

He shakes his head. "Unless you have a kindred blood running around"—he waves a dismissive palm at the general vicinity of her domicile—"there is no chance. Gunnar allowed himself to be pierced by the blade, and I fear his secondary heart has been punctured. If it was his main heart"—Slade shrugs—"he would survive much, but this is too grievous a wound for him to battle without blood from a kindred."

"What the hell is a 'kindred'? And for the record"—Jacky points at Slade—"aren't these the bad guys?"

Beth nods. "Yes, but this Bloodling is my father."

"Well…*shit*," Jacky says.

"Yes," Beth answers, holding the hand of the male she'd beaten up a scant hour ago. She's done so much crying in the last day, she can't remember what it was like to live her entire life with dry eyes.

Her sadness soaks Gunnar, and she wipes the tears angrily from her cheeks.

Maddie slowly moves forward as Slade stands silently and Jeb holds the wound he has at his shoulder.

"You're hurt, too." Beth pries his hand away. The flesh is punctured with five holes—talons—and the surrounding skin is an angry scarlet.

Beth's attention moves to Gunnar, whose breath is labored. Beth hangs her head. Covering her eyes with her forearm, she sobs into her shirtsleeve.

I can't believe I've found him only to lose him. And by Jeb's hand.

"I think I can help," a feminine voice says.

"Impossible," Slade says with quiet wonder. It's the first time since Beth's seen him that his voice has held any emotion.

Beth looks at Maddie and meets wide midnight-blue eyes. Her gaze is slightly vacant, as though she's acting under compulsion.

Gunnar's eyes snap open, like black luster in a face chalky with death.

"My kindred blood," he whispers.

Maddie nods, seemingly without fear of the huge Bloodling and she scoots between the end of the couch and where Beth crouches.

"What's going on?" Jacky asks, looking around at everyone.

"Don't let him hurt me," Maddie says dreamily. Then she lies sideways across Gunnar's chest, her neck bare to his lips. His large hand covers the side of her head.

"I shall not hurt you," Gunnar says with deliberate slowness, and it's obvious to Beth that he's using the last of his energy to speak.

"Ah no, not digging this sacrificial lamb thing." Jacky moves forward, and Slade grabs him by the back of his neck, lifting him off the floor. His legs swing. "Let me down, ya clown!"

Slade doesn't, and Maddie scoots closer to Gunnar's mouth.

"Madeline…" Jeb moves forward as though to stop her.

Gunnar strikes deep. His jaws move as Maddie's blood flows into his mouth, and his throat begins to convulse as he draws deep.

"Slade—stop him. He'll kill her," Beth says. She and Jeb didn't bring Maddie to Papilio for her safety, only to subject her to a death by the hands of a One.

"He will not. Watch, tiny frog."

Beth watches, forgetting to be annoyed by the endearment.

Color floods Gunnar's cheeks, then his hand rises. He yanks the blade from his chest and tosses it aside.

After another minute, he sits up, pulling Maddie more deeply into his embrace, cradling her in his lap.

His ebony eyes look out over the audience in challenge. His look says what his mouth can't—that he'll kill all comers.

"Please, Gunnar, don't kill Madeline. She…she has nothing. Only this wretched life, not one thing more." Beth beseeches him with her eyes.

Gunnar pulls from her neck, one finger absently stroking her skin. Finally, he takes his lips off her throat and licks every last drop off his mouth.

Maddie's head falls back, and she appears to rest against the crook of his arm. He runs a tongue over the twin puncture wounds, and they begin to close.

"Let me down, freak!" Jacky bellows. "That vamp fucker needs to get his creepy fangs away from Maddie."

"They are out, Three slime," Slade counters.

"Slade," Beth says, giving a cautious look at Maddie, who's not been killed. Then she shifts her gaze to her newfound father, whose wound has stopped bleeding and is already healing. "Let Jacky down."

"Gladly," Slade says in disgust.

He releases Jacky, who falls to the floor with the grace of a wet cat.

"Dick," he says, scooting away.

Slade looks ready to do more, so Beth jumps between them. "Don't. It's a volatile time."

"Volatile?" Jeb asks from the ground. He indicates Maddie with a hand. "A One just took blood from our charge, and I did nothing to protect her because he is your father. Look how far we've come."

Slade shakes his head. "She is fine. A finite number of females have kindred blood with one of our kind. That this one would show up here at just the right time is beyond coincidence. It is a favor issued by fate."

Jacky's eyebrows rise. "Kind of like the lottery?" He's sullenly interested.

Beth feels better that another crisis seems to have been averted.

Slade's eyebrows come together, and Beth allows a small smile. "Jacky means the chances of such a female would be small," she explains.

"Infinitesimal," Slade confirms.

Jacky snaps a thumb at Gunnar and Maddie. "So what does that mean?"

"It means that she is his, technically," Slade recites blandly.

It's too much for Beth, and she sits on the nearest chair, hard. If the seat hadn't been there, she would have landed on her ass.

Maddie lies in Gunnar's arms like a small child, and he strokes the hair back from her face.

"Eff this noise." Jacky strides toward the pair with clear intent etched on his features.

Gunnar's head whips to the young Three and he hisses. Fangs lengthen, venom sparkling at the tips.

"Not scared, vamp dude—bring it." Jacky grabs a bronze sculpture off a low table in front of the couch and hoists it to his shoulder. "Let Maddie go or I'm going to pretend I need a home run with your head as the baseball."

Gunnar stands with Maddie in his arms.

"Drop that or die." His words are slightly muffled through the fangs, but Beth hears the warning.

Jacky smirks. "Putz." Then he's closing the distance, the heaviest part of the statue poised to brain Beth's father.

She does the only thing she can.

14

Jeb

Unreal.

Beth's foot whips out in front of Jacky, and down he goes, sending the statue flying.

Jeb jumps to his feet and grabs the hurtling sculpture.

Slade moves forward, presumably to punish the boy.

"Don't, Bloodling. Leave him. He's doing what he thinks is right." Jeb's tone clearly says that Slade's done nothing right.

He scowls then glances at Beth, pale and exhausted in the chair. He steps down.

Jacky picks himself up and gives Beth a dirty look. "Thanks a lot—that sucked."

"Sorry," Beth says. "I thought things were going south in a hurry."

Jacky jerks his thumb at Gunnar. "So your pop gets to fang Maddie and do whatever he wants?" Jackie folds his arms.

Beth leans forward, putting her forearms on her thighs. "No," she says softly, hands dangling between her legs.

Jacky turns in a slow circle, taking them all in. "Am I the only one here getting the big picture?"

Gunnar's fangs have retracted and Maddie seems to have come around. "Big picture?" Gunnar asks and Jacky nods.

"Madeline is—she's been through a lot and she doesn't need to be some blood concubine or something because you're hungry and shit."

"I was dying, Three."

"It's Jacky you fanged fucktard."

"Jacky," Maddie chastises softly then she taps Gunnar's shoulder. "Would you, can you let me down?"

Gunnar nods but adds, "Stay close to me."

Maddie smiles. "I—these guys aren't going to hurt me." Her hand goes to where Gunnar took blood.

He lets Maddie slip down the front of him, and even Jeb tenses at the huge size disparity. Maddie comes to well below his shoulder, looking positively fragile beside the nearly seven-feet-tall Bloodling.

He cradles her face, kissing her forehead, each cheek, then her mouth.

Maddie stands still, her eyes still closed seconds after his lips have left her face. "Wow," she breathes.

"Maddie," Jacky says sharply, and she startles, turning to him. "Don't let him vamp you. He's got some weird mojo, I'll admit..."

"It doesn't work on males," Slade comments dryly.

Jacky pushes his longish hair out of his face. "Thank fuck."

Kennet chuckles. "You do have a way with Three words."

Jacky screws up his face. "Yeah. Duh—they're mine." He rolls his eyes.

Kennet frowns and Jeb feels a grin stretch his face. He has to admit, Jacky somehow adds a perverse balance to a barely tolerable circumstance.

"Maddie, can you get away from him?" Jacky points at Gunnar.

She nods. "Sure." She begins to walk away from him and Gunnar says, "Thank you."

Color swamps Maddie's cheekbones and she whispers, "Welcome."

Beth walks to Maddie. "I'm sorry, Maddie. I—I just found out Gunnar is my father."

She shakes her head slightly. "I can tell. You guys feel alike."

Jeb frowns. "What do you mean?"

Maddie lifts a shoulder. Her newly trimmed dark brown hair slides over her shoulders, landing in the hollow between her shoulder blades. "I can't explain it very well. I walked in here, and I could feel his need," she swallows, casting a shy glance at Gunnar. "I had to answer."

"Seems like a big old user to me," Jacky mumbles, his eyes narrowing on Gunnar.

"That's great you have a dad," she says, her eyes dropping.

Jacky appears to guess her thoughts. "Screw Chuck, Maddie. That turd is gone forever."

She nods quickly, her fingers wiping tears as fast as they fall. "Yeah."

"Who is this Chuck?" Gunnar asks, moving toward Maddie.

"Back off," Jacky says.

Gunnar snorts. "No one tells me what to do, Three."

"Jacky, asshole," he corrects without fear of reprisal and Beth's eyes close.

"Jacky," Jeb begins, "we'll figure out this situation better if you're not using every bit of profanity you possess."

A crooked smile flashes across his face. "I'm not even warmed up yet, Merrick."

Kennet chuckles. "The boy has a point. Bloodlings are the natural enemies of Reflectives. He's taken blood from a female under our care." Kennet plants his feet apart, folding his arms, and gives Slade a hard stare. "Explain what's going on, Bloodling."

"Yeah, park it for awhile guys and expound on your unwanted presence." Jacky flops down on a recliner, spinning it in a single revolution.

"Jacky," Maddie says, "quit it."

Jacky pops up again and walks the short distance to Maddie. He grabs her arm and shakes her slightly. "Nah. These guys need their feet held to the fire, as my pop would say."

"Take your hands from the female, Three."

Jacky looks at Gunnar and Jeb intervenes. "They are both from Three. Madeline and Jacky have known each other since they were younglings."

"He cannot touch her."

Jacky grins. "Y'know, you're sure owning a lot of shit that's not yours. Back off."

Gunnar moves in a blur of pearl-gray air rushing past Jeb.

Then he's got Jacky by the throat.

Maddie screams and steps between them, putting her palms on Gunnar's chest. "Please, I love him—Jacky's all the family I have."

Gunnar hisses, dropping Jacky, who lands on his ass for the second time, hands at his throat.

Gunnar grips Maddie against his chest. "Don't hurt him—please," she repeats.

Gunnar's hand moves below her hair, kneading her nape softly. "For you I will abstain."

"What's going on, Jeb?" Beth asks.

Jeb moves toward her and away from the couple forming before his eyes.

"What is this complication, Merrick?" Kennet asks, looking between Gunnar and Maddie then at Slade.

Jeb takes Beth's hand, and a low growl parts Slade's lips. Jeb gives him a sharp look.

"I think," Jeb says slowly, "that we have two Bloodlings that are here for a purpose, and Maddie's been caught in some kind of blood magic."

Jacky coughs. "I think it's a shit ton more than that, Merrick. Did you hear the big doofus?" He hitches his jaw toward Slade. "He said that Maddie was this other slack jaw's."

"What is a 'slack jaw'?" Gunnar asks, his eyes pinning Jacky to the floor.

Beth groans.

"Don't explain, Jacky," Jeb says.

"A dumb ass," Jacky answers, smirking.

"Jacky," Maddie says, "I'm begging you—stop egging him on."

"No begging, small one," Gunnar says, stroking a finger underneath her chin. "You beg to no one."

Jacky snorts. "You don't know Maddie, chump. All you needed right then was a quick bite." Jacky snaps his teeth together several times, and both Gunnar and Slade glare at him. "And Maddie was conveniently here. No, she's just some—no offense, man—blood whore for you. And when another chick comes along with the yum factor, Maddie will be a throwaway. And dude, she doesn't need your brand of noise."

Beth moves with the speed of calculation, slapping her father's face so hard it rocks back. "You're a liar. Jacky's right."

Maddie cries out.

Jeb moves in as Gunnar grabs her wrist. "I am Bloodling. We are many things, but deceit at the expense of a defenseless female is not one of them."

A shrill whistle pierces the tense tangle of limbs and rage-filled gazes. All eyes move to Kennet.

His fingers drop from his lips. "I understand this is a huge mess. But what we really need to consider is all the Reflectives coming to collect Beth."

Jeb looks at Kennet, leaking a rough exhale. He nods. Kennet's right.

"*Who* is coming to take Beth?" Slade asks, his eyebrows gone low over glittering obsidian eyes.

"You don't need an explanation, Bloodling. She is my claimed soul mate. I am the only male who needs to understand Beth's future."

Beth blanches, and Jeb winces at his own words, however true they are.

Slade's lips curl. "Yes, and has she claimed you as well, Reflective?"

Jeb squares off with Slade, hearing Beth's sigh.

"Jeb," Beth says, touching his arm. Softening instantly at her touch, he flicks his eyes at her. "This isn't helping. Posturing is delaying. Kennet is trying to tell us to formulate a plan. Now."

She turns to Slade. "How much did you hear when you took me from The Cause Headquarters courtyard?"

Slade lifts his shoulders and Beth looks at Gunnar. "Nothing, we came upon you, and made the jump."

Beth gives him a sad smile. "Artful jumping, by the way." He inclines his head and Beth frowns. "I'm still mad as a hornet at you."

His lips curl. "As I said before, this is not the reunion I had planned."

"Wait a sec—" Jacky looks from Gunnar to Beth. "You didn't know you had a kid?"

Gunnar gives a slight shake of his head. "No."

"Well this is an epic fuck-up."

Slade holds up a palm in Jacky's direction, and his mouth snaps shut. "Be that as it may, I'll ask a second time—why are the Reflectives coming for Beth?" His eyes blaze at Jeb.

Jeb's shame is acute, but he refuses to sugarcoat the truth. "She is the only Reflective female on Papilio."

Slade and Gunnar take on identical expressions of horrific understanding.

"Did you publicly claim her, Reflective?" Slade asks.

Jeb inhales deeply.

"Did you?" Slade asks through his teeth.

"Yes," Jeb bites back.

"Yet, they still come for her?" Gunnar asks in a tone filled with menace.

Jeb nods. "We've been without leadership for five years." He swivels to Slade. "You know what Dimitri has done with our Reflectives. What Lance Ryan did. They overthrew The Cause—ousted Rachett. Then Ryan was the defunct leader of a corrupt and debauched order."

"And the females?" Gunnar's brows collide.

"They've been jumped to other sectors."

"What?" Shocked, Slade drops his hands to his sides.

Jeb nods. "Beth is the only female left. We need these male Reflectives to locate the females and bring them safely back. But there is no cohesive leadership and Ryan remains at large."

Slade throws his head back and laughs.

Jeb doesn't see the humor and his body tenses. Beth squeezes his hand.

"I have an idea, since your world is even more convoluted than ours."

Jeb smirks. "I doubt there's anything you can offer. I wager your very presence on Papilio has made things worse." He doesn't add Gunnar to the comment but his inference hangs in the air between them.

Gunnar holds Maddie loosely. "As I see it, you don't have many options. Your leader is missing, while another schemes in a dark corner somewhere. My daughter has made no claim on a male." He shrugs.

Jeb fights not to pull Beth against him.

"And Beth's life is in danger from her own kind. Really," he says, looking at Kennet, Jacky, and Jeb with mild distaste, "you do not understand the treasure you have in females, and you do not appear prepared to protect them properly."

"Not all guys are dicks to girls," Jacky says in sullen defense.

"There certainly aren't many prevalent examples in this sector," Slade comments in a dry voice.

Nobody argues.

Jeb swallows his pride as thoughts of keeping Beth safe fill his head. He can't outrun the entire Reflective command—or even most of them. "What do you suggest?" he finally asks Slade.

Jacky balks. "Merrick?! Come *on*!"

"Quiet, Jacky." Jeb's eyes are steady on Slade's.

Slade doesn't hesitate. "We jump to One."

"Merrick—Principle no—that would be so wrong," Kennet says.

Triumph, and something else Jeb can't discern, is written all over Gunnar's face.

Jeb glances at Kennet and shakes his head. "We need to think of Beth—and Maddie. We can't protect them. Not at present."

Kennet's mouth closes with a snap, and Calvin, so silent until now, blows out his disgust in a harsh exhale.

"Let's do it," Beth says, and Jeb wants to kiss her. She's the bravest person he's ever known.

"What about the other women?" Maddie asks from the shadow of Gunnar's form.

Jeb's eye flick in Maddie's direction. "We'll secure the women at One, and when things are more settled, we'll return here and galvanize groups to seek the females."

"Bad choices—all," Calvin says and Kennet nods assent.

Jeb shoots them a hard look. "Do either of you have anything better?"

Beth steps in front of him, gripping his shoulders. He sinks into her dark eyes.

"It's okay. It's all we have. Sometimes the best choice comes from terrible ones."

Beth turns to Slade. "What about Dimitri?"

A shadow passes over Slade's features, and a shiver of foreboding threads through Jeb. "I'll handle him."

"This is going to blow," Jacky says, following the others to find a safe place to jump.

For once, Jeb agrees with Jacky.

15

Beth can't believe how much her life has changed in a month's time. First, she endured the horrible induction courtesy of Reflective Ryan, when she had to jump to save her own skin.

Then she was paired with Jeb Merrick—womanizer, expert jumper, and warrior—only to have him claim her as his soul mate. Beth feels like at any moment, she'll wake up from a nightmare.

Their last jump to dispatch the woman-abusing Chuck and return thirteen-year-old Jacky to Three went up in smoke when Ryan disrupted the time continuum, moving Papilio time ahead of sector Three.

Ryan jumped the Reflective women before being assessed and brought back to a semblance of health. And Jacky aged to eighteen cycles. Just those two facts make Beth's head buzz.

Then her Bloodling father suddenly appears in her shattered world by sheer coincidence. She can't evaluate it all too closely, or she'll go crazy.

They have a saying about coincidence on Papilio: coincidence is destiny asserting its dominance.

Beth hasn't told Jeb her worries. She's angry at Gunnar. He holds the secrets to her mother—and Beth's unlikely beginnings. He also took blood from a willing Maddie.

Jeb thought the worst of Gunnar after she was responsible for freeing him of his pants.

The recent memory makes her chuckle, and Jeb gives her an inquisitive glance as they walk toward a lake buried in the deepest part of the forest behind her domicile.

"Oh—you remember how Gunnar didn't have any pants?" Beth's lips curl.

Jeb's face holds the grim look it usually does, and not for the first time, Beth wonders why he's always so serious. Of course, their situation currently warrants it, and her laughter dies.

"Unforgettable," he remarks, keeping his eyes on Slade and Gunnar as they travel ahead. He glances behind him in silent communication with Kennet and Calvin as they hold the rear position.

"Well, they slipped me something."

Jeb stalls, turning to her. "What do you mean?" His hands go to his hips.

He's not going to like this. "They drugged me."

Jeb whirls, striding fast toward the Bloodlings just ahead.

Beth grabs him. *Hothead.* "Jeb—no," she whisper-hisses.

He looks down at her hand, and she can see the influence her touch has over him. His shoulders relax, and his eyes soften as he gazes down at her.

"Why?" his lips thin. "Tell me this instant, or I kill them both. Father or not."

Beth folds her arms, throwing a hip out. "I was under the influence of whatever it was…"

"You weren't metabolizing it?" Jeb's eyebrow quirks.

"No—I'm half-Reflective, remember," she says in a low voice.

Beth watches Jeb put the pieces together. "Slade isn't here for reconnaissance," he says slowly.

Beth shakes her head. "I don't trust him. But that male"—she points at Gunnar—"*is* my father. And, Jeb, he could have killed me. He is amply skilled."

Jeb looks after their broad backs, now two dwindling specks. One of the specks stops, and a face turns to regard their delay.

His face fills with suspicion. "Are you certain he's your father?"

Beth's lips flatten. "Yes, and I unwound his weapons tether as a distraction."

"Ah," Jeb says in semi-understanding, and a reluctant smile passes for humor across his lips.

"She pants-ed him," Jacky remarks, moving by them and eavesdropping along the way.

Jeb groans, glaring at Jacky's retreating back. "I can't take much more of this."

"Tough," Jacky throws back as he keeps trekking up the steep incline. "You're stuck with my amazing ass."

Jeb frowns after him, and Beth grabs Jeb's arm. He returns his attention to her.

"Let's go. I don't want them suspicious. We follow them to One. We avoid the slaver—"

"Dimitri?"

"Yes. We get Maddie somewhere safe…"

"And you?" Jeb asks, touching her cheek.

Beth flushes beneath his fingertips.

Jeb visibly controls his breathing. His pupils dilate, those stormy eyes missing nothing.

The silence lengthens as he studies her with a hooded gaze.

"I want you. I can't pretend in your presence, Beth."

Beth stares, taking in all the signs of his arousal, and is too honorable to dismiss it. "I know."

"It can't be helped, Beth."

Reflectives were taught about the power of the soul mate bond. Beth inhales deeply. "Not good timing, Jeb. And for the record, I still can't believe I'm the one." She laughs nervously and casts a furtive glance at the Bloodlings, who are hiking back to Jeb and Beth's position.

Jeb ignores everyone but her, moving closer still, until their bodies are touching lightly.

"Please, Beth," Jeb's large hands come down on her shoulders, and she looks up into his eyes.

Jeb is so handsome, looking at him is almost hypnotic. Beth's never really allowed herself the luxury of studying his face. Her eyes trace every chiseled feature. His light gray eyes appear luminescent in the vague light between the open meadow and the deeper part of the woods that begin at the crest of the hill where they stand.

Beth reaches up tentatively and runs her fingers through his newly shorn dark-blond hair. Jeb leans into her caress, folding her smaller body against his own.

They fit together so perfectly, Beth gives a little moan of deep pleasure.

Reflectives are after her. She and Slade have unfinished business. Her father holds more secrets than truths. She understands all this, but Beth will always be that lone female in her mind, abused and unloved, even in the arms of a pureblood Reflective male she could never have dreamed of being with.

Jeb's lips come down on hers. They're as light as a feather and as deep as a bottomless pool. His hands warm the small of her back, his fingers spreading at the hollow as he presses her against him.

Her hands creep behind his neck.

Each second, she feels the heat of her kinship with her father grow as he moves closer.

Yet she doesn't stop what's happening between Jeb and her.

His hands close on her ribs, and he lifts her, crushing her against him. Her hands move to his face, hard beneath her fingertips, his mouth so tender against her lips.

"Jeb," she breathes against him.

"I know." Reluctantly, he releases her, setting her gently on the ground. He taps his forehead against hers then turns to face the approaching Bloodlings.

Slade stomps toward them, and Beth moves to stand in front of Jeb.

His face is contained thunder. "You delay us."

"You don't own me, Slade," Beth says.

Jeb moves to go around her, and she stays him. She will never hide behind a man. Beth is a Reflective, and this Bloodling will not harm her. She doesn't trust Slade's motivations, but she doesn't think hurting her is within him.

Slade smiles, and Beth fights not to squirm beneath a gaze that feels as though it bores holes into her very soul, ripping apart the sinew from the marrow, separating her heart from her mind.

Beth's breaths grow shallow as they stare at each other. Her body heats.

"Beth," Jeb calls, and he sounds worried, faraway.

Slade moves slowly toward her, and Beth sways. Even as Jeb's kisses burn on her lips, she feels the pull to Slade.

"What's happening?" Beth asks softly as though in a stupor.

"Blood call," Slade replies in his smooth voice. "All female Bloodlings will respond to an unmated male."

Beth hears his words then shakes out of the strange thrall.

Jeb is holding her arms, his own looped through hers.

"What—what happened?" she asks in a voice that doesn't sound like hers.

Jeb shakes his head. "I don't know, but one minute you were"—he glares at Slade—"with me."

Her embarrassment flares to life again.

"And in the next, you were going to him. Not like it was a choice, but as though you were in a trance."

Beth relaxes against Jeb. He's safe. Reliable.

Her eyes narrow to slits of distrust. "You're using Bloodling trickery."

Slade leans forward, and Jeb pulls Beth backward.

He grins, his dark eyes locking with Beth's gaze. "It is *no* trick."

Without another word, he turns back to where Gunnar stands beside Maddie.

Beth watches his fluid departure and shivers. "I am starting to rethink this jump, Jeb."

"I hear you, Beth." Jeb turns her slowly in the opposite direction and points to where they came from.

Beth can just make out the roof of her domicile, a flat black square floating over the rolling hills they just traversed.

Movement catches her eye. There are people there, moving like ants over a favorite hill. Many.

The Reflectives have come.

"Jeb…" Beth clutches her stomach. Panic spreads through her belly like a moth's wings.

"We can't fight them all, Beth," Jeb says softly. "I need to get you somewhere safe until there's new leadership."

"They must hate me so much," Beth says sadly as she watches them scurry around her home.

But Jeb surprises her by shaking his head. "It's not hate."

Their eyes meet.

"It's want," he says with grim certainty.

Jeb grabs her hand, and they quickly hike the hill, following after the Threes and Bloodlings.

She glances back once. The ants appear bigger.

Beth's never been so happy for the lack of reflections between here and her domicile.

16

Merrick

Lake Crystalline isn't crystal at all. Lily pads are scattered about its edges like a hasty sewing job done by Mother Nature. A sluggish spring beneath the lake feeds just enough fresh water for it not to stagnate, leaving it murky, its depths uncertain.

Kennet and Calvin jog to Jeb and Beth's position. Jeb glances at them then shifts his gaze to Beth, who is deep in conversation with Maddie.

The discussion looks heated.

The Bloodlings stand together, and Jeb questions the decision to jump to One again. His ears catch the muted sounds of stealth.

His fellow Reflectives approach while he second-guesses all the choices he has—and the ones he doesn't.

Reflecting to One is the best choice among bad ones.

They *could* jump to another sector other than One. But the Reflectives advancing upon them will not be as willing to go to One. There, they would be outnumbered by nightlopers and right back in the mess they'd fought their way out of. Jeb thinks they'll forgo that honor.

Kennet claps him on the back. "I used the pulsen-oculars. Ryan is not among them."

Some of the tension riding his shoulders eases with the news. However, Ryan's absence just means he could crop up like a weed somewhere else, most likely when Jeb needs him the least.

"Principle dammit."

Kennet gives a grim nod, folding his arms. Calvin keeps vigil over the growing contingent of Reflectives behind them.

"How long?" Jeb gives him a sharp glance.

Calvin's brow knots, worry on every line of his face. "Five minutes or so."

They need the wind at their backs from a jump. They should not be standing around, discussing the shit reflection offered by Lake Crystalline.

Slade and Gunnar approach, and Jeb automatically assesses them. *Six feet, seven. Two hundred eighty pounds. IQ one hundred thirty-five.* His eyes sweep to Slade. *One hundred forty for him.*

Jeb scowls; a smart enemy is a challenge.

"Picking us apart, Reflective?" Gunnar's inky eyes rake over Jeb.

He doesn't bother answering with a lie. "Yes. I am Reflective."

"Save the spiel," Slade says, raising a hand to ward off Jeb's words before he can utter them. "We both understand the esteem in which you all hold yourselves."

His obvious disdain for The Cause makes Jeb's blood boil.

"Then you should understand how deadly serious we are about seeing The Cause through."

Slade's and Jeb's gazes collide. The Bloodling parts his lips with an almost-inaudible hiss.

Beth walks up with Maddie and Jacky. She looks between the two of them and says, "We don't have time for male posturing."

Jacky points a finger at Jeb and Slade. "Y'know…"

"Quiet, Jacky," Kennet says.

He flips his bangs out of his sweaty face, kicking a loose pebble toward the sludge of the shore. "If we had some more chicks here, there'd be enough hens to offset all the roosters. Yeah."

Everyone ignores him.

"This is the best reflection we have." Jeb looks at Gunnar, who jumped using rushing water, and cocks an eyebrow, asking silently for confirmation he can jump the group.

"For proximity," Beth adds.

Gunnar shrugs. "It can be done, though it is blind water."

Blind water means that the Reflective cannot see where it will take a jumper. Ascribing a human sense to an inanimate object is not uncommon, but it is odd to hear Reflective phrases and references coming from Gunnar the Bloodling. Judging from Beth's expression, his words strike her the same way.

"I'd give anything to go back to Earth," Jacky comments sullenly.

"Too risky," Kennet says, frowning. "Every Reflective who follow us can jump that in their sleep."

"You guys just have the one lake on a shifter world?" Jacky asks in the general direction of the Bloodlings.

"Sector One," Beth corrects automatically.

Jacky shrugs, tossing his long bangs again. "God. Okay, let's get this over with and get our asses kicked in the sandbox, because—yeah—it was so fun before."

Maddie shyly takes Jacky's hand, and Gunnar's brows drop over his black eyes.

Jacky stares him down. "She's my friend, so back off." Gunnar looks as if he's about to say something. "She's not into violence. Ya dig? So there are no points for you vamping all over my ass. Just saying." He scowls at Gunnar.

Jeb interrupts, "We need to jump or stay and fight."

Gunnar silently walks to Beth and holds out his large hands. After a moment's pause, she slides hers inside his.

Jeb slides a finger through her belt loop, and Kennet places his hands on Maddie. Calvin does the same on Jacky.

Slade rests his hand on Gunnar's shoulder, and Jeb focuses all his anger on Slade.

His answering smile mocks Jeb.

Jeb looks away as familiar heat engulfs his feet. A slow smolder rises up his legs and flings itself to his extremities. He gifts his reflective energy to Beth, as do Kennet and Calvin. The power of the jump swamps their small party as it passes from person to person in a loop.

Jeb hears the Reflectives crashing through the brush that borders the lake, and he scoops out the last of his energy from deep inside, trusting Beth. Trusting her as one would a partner.

The water is suddenly much clearer. And Jeb's next breath is heat edged in ice.

His lungs buck at the familiar beginnings of the jump, then the lake rushes toward him—but not all of it, just the tips of the barest of the waves. Tired sunlight strikes their undulating movement and is refracted back at them.

Beth and Gunnar grab the shattered reflections and share the power among the ones who can't jump.

The noise falls away as the roar of the jump overwhelms the sound of Jeb's own blood pumping in his veins. Their collective power snaps like a finely honed instrument, and Jeb moves his hold from Beth's belt loop to her hip.

Fire and ice assail them from all sides, then they're falling onto the beach on One. He thought he'd never revisit the sector. Jeb's first searing breath chills, and on the second, he stands, taking in the view of a lake much clearer than Lake Crystalline. This one sparkles like captured diamonds.

"It's so pretty," Maddie says, gazing around.

Gunnar moves up behind her and rests his hand at her neck with familiarity that Jeb doesn't like. "There is much beauty in this sector."

Jacky snorts, and Maddie gives him a vague frown. "Listen, Mad, maybe vamp dude is kinda hot—I don't know—but this place"—Jacky gestures around him at the arid and mountainous region—"has got some bad juju."

Her eyes dance nervously around them, as though monsters might tear out of the ground at their feet. "Is it worse than Papilio?" she asks.

Kennet, Calvin, Beth, and Jeb exchange looks full of mutual regret. There was a time when Papilio would have been hailed as the safest and most moral sector of all.

It's a claim they can no longer make.

"Yes," Jeb says, because it's true. The Reflectives they left behind have lost focus without Rachett. Still, night-lopers and Bloodlings don't run rampant in his home world.

Jeb looks to Gunnar and Slade to defend their sector. But Jeb's earlier intellectual assessment holds true. Both Bloodlings are of superior intellect and avoid entering into a pissing match.

Gunnar tilts Maddie's chin up and looks deeply into her eyes. "It is true; Papilio is dangerous in a way it was not before. However, there are creatures here without code or honor."

Slade's faces harden at the other male's words, but he doesn't deny it—because he can't.

"I want to go to Earth," Maddie admits quietly, then sucks her lip between her teeth to quiet its trembling.

Jacky jerks his arms dramatically, letting his hands slap his thighs.

Kennet gives him a look of warning.

Gunnar shakes his head slowly. "No, little hopper. The big bad hoppers will surely follow you there. Have they not discovered you are capable of jumping?"

Maddie appears too shaken by all the change to notice Gunnar's overt condescension, and she shakes her head. "No. I came to Papilio, Ryan went crazy, and I *hid*. I don't think anyone had time to identify what I was. And now, I'm not just a Dimensional. I'm a jumper—Reflective—whatever. And some blood thingy, too."

Gunnar's brows pop. "A blood thingy?"

Maddie nods.

"Three lingo, dude. Catch up." Jacky seems to consider, thumb to chin. "Or maybe just chick chat. Yeah."

Jeb fumes. *Threes.*

"A hidden female Reflective in their midst," Slade says thoughtfully, ignoring Jacky's sideline comments.

"So there's two of you?" Slade asks, glancing between Beth and Maddie.

Beth nods. "Madeline is untrained, and she has been through a lot for someone so young." Beth doesn't expound on the atrocities of the young woman's childhood.

"I hate to break it to you guys, and *I* shouldn't be the one thinking about our mutual protection and that, but I think we've got company. Time to move to plan B."

Jeb whirls, and the air above the lake grows heavy, lit with obscure opaque vapor.

"They follow," Gunnar says, eyeing the coalescence that precedes a jump.

"Someone is." Maddie backs away from the lapping water.

"Come." Slade sprints up the sand dune embankment.

Beth and Jeb look at each other, a silent hesitation gripping them both. In the end, they run after him. Jacky and the two Reflective warriors follow closely at their heels.

Gunnar swings Maddie onto his back with a stern, "Hold on."

Seagrass-like fronds beat at Jeb's pants as he moves swiftly up the incline and crests the hill.

Despite the uphill run, no one is panting. All the species are in top condition; even Jacky seems to flourish on One.

Together, they turn, checking to see who follows.

Jeb couldn't be more shocked.

"Oh, my Principle!" Beth cries, rushing pell-mell back down the embankment.

"Beth! No!"

Jeb has no choice but to chase after her.

Three Reflective females plunge out of the middle of the sky and into a lake. Their screams of sheer terror echo over the relative quiet of the water.

Jeb flinches, knowing their horror is like a dinner bell for nightlopers. He gauges the time of day, thanking Principle it's only the start of twilight.

Triple moons bleed wan light over the women. They flail and scream, their wide eyes pitching around for anything solid, familiar.

None can swim.

The others race back to the shore, heedless of who might follow.

Jeb has only the Eighth hammering in his brain: *Defend those who cannot.*

The group leaps into the icy lake to save those who cannot save themselves.

17

Beth

Beth took her Reflective training seriously and is well-versed in all sorts of different pursuits not relevant to Papilio. This includes swimming.

Reflecting is so entrenched in the Papilion culture that the few lakes that exist are rarely used to jump, and even less likely to be used to swim. There are so many portals, large and small, that reflect, the papiliones have little use for swimming.

That's why the three Reflective females, assigned to clerical, are currently drowning.

Beth heaves herself into the lake without hesitation, and her boots weigh her down immediately. Using a Three swimming stroke, aptly named "the butterfly," she tosses her body out of the water, launching back with persistent accuracy.

Jeb uses the "crawl" and gains on the drowning women. Being an expert swimmer was one of the only things that saved Beth in the lake when she and Ryan jumped together.

It would be the only thing to save the women—if she could get to them.

She breaks the surface of the frigid water, takes a wild sucking breath, and sees a pale hand waving like a frantic flag above the surface.

Beth dives, shooting underneath the water and stabbing toward the lone limb.

She grabs the woman about the waist then surges backward and up. They bob along the surface like an unlikely buoy, and Beth gasps.

Kennet and Jeb grab the remaining two. One woman is not breathing. Calvin is waiting on shore, ready to assist.

Beth's spluttering charge fights Beth, possibly still assuming she's drowning.

Her struggling begins to cause Beth to sink. Beth turns her head to suck air, driving her right arm back as she pulls behind her, using her powerful legs to kick backward.

The woman elbows her in the stomach, and Beth folds, going under. When she breaks the surface, she's dazed.

Oxygen deprivation.

Where the hades are Slade and Gunnar? I could use a little help.

Beth hazards a glance behind her and spots the Bloodlings pacing the shore, their unnervingly distraught eyes on her.

Why aren't they helping?

The same elbow strikes Beth hard in the nose, and blood pumps into the water, spreading around them.

Dizziness sinks its teeth into Beth's skull. "Stop!" Beth yells at the woman, and she stills.

Too late.

Unconsciousness slides into the pockets of her mind.

"Beth!" Jeb roars from somewhere close by.

Her hold on the woman loosens. *Dear Principle.*

Jeb can't reach her—he's got his own woman to save. They'll all go down.

"Slade!" Beth calls weakly. She reaches out, winding her fingers in the woman's hair, and yanks her by the scalp, driving toward shore.

"Ah!" she screams.

Beth's lips curl into a dazed smile. *That's what you get for fighting your rescuer.*

Beth rolls over, blowing water out of her mouth, and looks at Gunnar and Slade.

Fools.

"Why aren't you chumps saving the day?" Jacky yells. "God, with all the manpower, you two stand around? Doy."

Jacky dives in, leaving the Bloodlings at the shore.

Beth goes under again. Her eyes catch a single reflection where the water creeps to shore, growing shallow and clear.

Beth's eyes latch on to the reflection, and she sees her own eyes stare back for the span of a blink.

It's enough.

She knows she's too weak to reflect, but she jumps anyway.

Opening her eyes, Beth finds she's beneath Jacky. Surprised, she gasps, dragging water into her lungs.

She can't breathe.

Strong arms tear her from the water.

"Beth!"

Jeb.

He sounds so worried.

Weight settles on her chest.

Her eyes bulge. *No air!*

Jeb and Slade peer down at her. Slade shoves Jeb, and he flies away.

Slade gazes down at her, cupping her face.

"Tiny frog." His teeth tear at his forearm.

Beth shakes her head, just the barest motion, and he smiles down at her.

No more of his blood.

The expression never reaches his eyes. He can't erase the worry from his features, no matter how hard he tries. Slade pretends around Jeb, but not when it's only her.

Hot blood splatters across Beth's face, and Jeb looms behind Slade.

Gunnar lays hands on Jeb, and they begin to beat each other with fists.

Kennet attacks Gunnar; Calvin joins in.

"Look only at me, tiny frog."

Beth's eyes roll frantically from Gunnar to Slade's depthless eyes.

I can't breathe, she tries to say. Opening her mouth allows his blood to enter hers, and Beth tastes it. The first drop, then the second.

It scalds her tongue.

She swallows, though she still can't breathe.

Beth's back arches off the sand. She chokes, coughing blood and lake water.

Slade moves her gently onto her side. He rubs his palm in slow circles over her back.

Beth's ashamed, but she reaches for the raw wound of his arm, taking what he offers. Sighing, she latches on then breaks away, coughing.

She strikes again, drinking deeply of his vein. When Beth is satiated, the sounds of fists against flesh recede, and she falls away.

"That is so disgusting!" Beth hears Jacky say, but her eyelids don't flicker.

Strong arms lift Beth, cradling her.

"Put her the fuck down."

Groaning ensues from below her.

"No." The hold tightens, and Beth knows she's safe. "Do not interrupt what I've done," Slade says.

"What you've done is tie her more strongly to you," Jeb growls.

"And what did you do, Reflective, but let your partner drown?"

"I was right there!" Jeb roars. "I had her, and she jumped to move closer to shore. If she had not, even now, she would be free of the poison of your veins."

Beth's eyes slowly open, and her hand falls out of Slade's embrace. She beckons with her hand, and after a hard look at Slade, Jeb comes.

"Don't," Beth coughs, and a bit of Slade's blood escapes her lips. She unselfconsciously licks it off. "He did what he could. I don't know what was causing the trouble. I couldn't tell—" She clears her throat, and Jeb takes her hand, resentment for Slade leaking from his pores. "I couldn't tell how far away you were. I figured we'd both drown."

"Bloodlings can't survive in water," Slade says.

Gunnar gets to his feet. His face is swelling from the attack from Kennet, Jeb, and Calvin. Maddie is crying softly in the background.

Jeb has the grace to cast his eyes away. "He was trying to keep me from you."

"I don't think he'd hurt me, Jeb. He just wanted to make sure I started breathing again, and Slade was making that happen."

Beth sits up straight.

"Slowly, tiny frog," Slade cautions.

"Where's the Reflective I saved?" Beth looks around frantically. "Did I save her?"

"Yes."

Beth turns her head in the direction of the voice.

She knows that voice.

Daphne.

Beth flops back against Slade, throwing an arm over her face.

Figures.

"I'm sorry. I know you hate me."

Beth's arm falls away, and she looks at the woman.

She doesn't look like the same highly coiffed Daphne of old. She looks like a barely put together, soaking-wet shell of who she used to be.

"I don't hate you," Beth lies.

She shrugs her narrow shoulders, looking at the ground. "I was one of the females who regularly made fun of you."

Beth lets out a deep breath. *True.*

She's about to be gracious after her near-drowning. "Maybe, but everything's different now, isn't it?"

Daphne nods, eyes still glued to the sand. "I can't swim. I didn't mean to…" She bursts into tears.

Maddie moves to her side, wrapping an arm around her shoulders. "We're all lucky Beth and Jeb came back."

Daphne's tear-stained face rises, and raw accusation lies in her wide, sea-green eyes. "Why did you ever leave us in the first place? Do you know what we are now?"

"Put me down," Beth says.

Slade sets her on her feet. He must sense she'll plant her face in the sand, because his grip remains firm.

Jeb moves to her side as Gunnar spits a wad of bloody mucus in the sand, eyeing the Reflectives warily.

"I know what Reflective Ryan did," Beth confirms in a low voice. "I know that it's a miracle you and the other two Reflectives managed to leave whatever sector you were in and coincidentally jump to where we happened to be. And I know that you don't have to be what he forced you to be anymore. We're not going anywhere."

Jeb takes Beth's hand again, and gives Slade a look that seems to clearly say, *I've got her now.*

Slade maintains his hold.

Beth gently drags the two behind her as she crosses the short distance to Daphne and Maddie.

The men are silent, even Jacky.

"The thing we accused you of, laughed at behind your back—we're so much worse, Reflective Jasper," Daphne says with a defeated laugh.

"Whores for The Cause."

Jeb releases Beth's hand, and she presses her fingers to the other woman's blue-tinged lips. "You are whores no longer. Choiceless no longer. Reflective Ryan will pay for his crimes, as will all those who share in the wrongdoing."

Daphne grips Beth's hands so tightly, the blood retreats from her fingers, leaving them ghostly pale.

Daphne blinks back her tears and gives a small nod.

The Cause was an absolute.

Now it's a broken ideal.

18

Slade

Jeb Merrick is a problem.

He's remained a burr in Slade's side since he was able to heal himself after his fight with Reflective Ryan.

Merrick will not go quietly. He's staked a claim on Beth, and though Bloodlings *do* have kindred bloods in the rare female from time to time, there is no such thing as a soul mate. It is a folktale among his ancestral Blood Singers on sector Seven and unheard of on One. Males and females form alliances merely to propagate the species. That is what is of critical importance to Bloodlings.

Romantic-soul-mate searching is for fools, and Slade is no fool. He will ignore the tenderness he feels for this tiny frog. He will conquer the weakness inside himself until it is soot in the bottom of a burning heart of hate.

He loathes Dimitri. The advantage he enjoyed during Gunnar's captivity has endangered all Bloodlings with the taking of their females.

"What troubles you?" Gunnar asks quietly as the group makes their way to the forests of the Bloodlings.

So much is deeply troubling, but he can convey none of it to Gunnar. Slade can just imagine the consequences of telling Gunnar the unvarnished truth.

Yes, Gunnar, your newly discovered warrior Reflective daughter of Lucinda, the love of your life? She is the price for the return of the remaining Bloodling females.

Slade would last a solid three minutes, at most.

Beth would be endangered.

Instead, Slade says, "Nothing, just that we be light on our feet and that we reach the tops of the great forest to secure the females."

Gunnar frowns, keeping his stride.

Slade can almost feel the older Bloodling weigh each one of his words—and he finds the comment wanting.

"What of my daughter?" he asks slowly.

Slade gives a minimal shrug, then ticks off the facts. "We assisted her escape. Their world is in turmoil. It was a mercy to help."

Gunnar grabs his arm, and Slade steels himself.

The mirrored black of Gunnar's irises flashes in the growing gloom. "I know there is something more. I understand our little hopper was here. She was nearly under the thumb of that derelict Reflective..."

"Ryan," Slade volunteers.

Gunnar nods, his eyes shifting toward the tight-knit group of Reflectives and threes not twenty paces behind him.

"This is not the safest sector for her."

It is not the safest sector for anyone. "She doesn't appear to like you," Slade states.

Gunnar shrugs. "Her liking me does not change what she means to me." His eyes glitter as his anger rises to the surface like oil in water. "She is the Bloodling daughter of Lucinda, and I'll not desert her as so many apparently have during her short life. I will defend Beth—as I did today when you gave her the restorative blood share." Gunnar viciously tightens his hair club, looking back at the group as they draw nearer. "The Reflectives who are pure blood do not understand what it is to be a Bloodling."

He has no idea. Slade remains in contemplative silence.

"When Dimitri gets his claws into me, he will try and imprison me again. We can't have that."

If Dimitri doesn't imprison him, Gunnar will kill me for giving up Beth.

"Ah!" Gunnar exclaims softly.

Slade follows Gunnar's gaze to the glowing lights in the canopy of the trees high above.

Gunnar claps Slade on his shoulder. "It is good to be home and not underneath a partially buried acre of stone."

Gunnar looks behind him and finds the male Three and Maddie. Slade has a moment of unease. Gunnar had better not start anything with the fragile Reflective. She has no strength of heart. Because she is from the chaotic sector of Three, Maddie is more liability than asset.

And she wishes to return to her home sector, not become a blood slave.

Yet kindred blood is indifferent to intellect and circumstance. It calls, and the ones under its magic answer.

Beth and the other Reflectives come to stand behind him, and Slade tilts his head to study the sky. He and Gunnar part their lips.

The call of the Bloodling, high and sharp, rises to rustle the leaves of their treetop homes.

Ropes unwind to fall head height.

Slade scans the lower trunks, so wide that five linked males would not surround the circumference.

Nothing. The wood is quiet.

Too quiet.

"Do you sense that?" Slade quickly asks Gunnar.

"Yes," he hisses, turning to the depth of the woods as Slade does.

The Reflectives take their silent cue, and Beth backs toward them, ceramic daggers in each hand. The blades point in opposite directions, traveling in a loose half-circle around her body.

"What is it? Nightlopers?" she asks with quiet intensity, her eyes boring into the darkness.

Slade nods.

"Jacky, Maddie, stand behind us," Jeb barks.

"Nightlopers—perfect, guys. Can't we get into the treehouses before we get in a catfight?"

"Jacky!" Maddie cries, and he sinks just as a paw swipes over his head. Strands of his hair float to the forest floor after the near-miss.

"Fuck a duck!" Jacky screeches. "That bastard about swiped my head off."

Nightlopers pour out of the womb of the surrounding forest. Partially furred bodies slink between one-thousand-year-old tree trunks.

Slade tallies their numbers, and the odds are not in his favor. He buries the instinct to protect Beth.

Merrick swings his blade and takes out much of the throat of the rat nightloper who swiped at the Three male.

Slade has a moment's regret that the Three made it before two lions come for him.

He slants his eyes at Beth and sees she is beside Gunnar. His talons punch painfully from his fingertips.

He flies over Maddie, who is huddling beside the Reflective females, and stabs his talons through the skull of the first lion. Impaling the five bony knives at his fingertips, he uses the nightloper as a tether and swings his left arm wide, catching the throat of the second.

His target staggers and stumbles forward, paws circling a throat oozing blood between his fingers.

Beth rushes to his aid, and he shouts, "No!" His fangs impede his pronunciation, and it comes out slurred.

Slade curses in frustration.

Beth ignores his warning. She jumps on his back, using it like a springboard.

She flies through the air, one leg curled beneath her body and one straight out, knives in her fists. "Ah!" she cries as she slams into a wolf nightloper.

Her foot gags his open mouth, and she wraps her free leg around his throat.

Slade stutters at the sight of Beth so close to the nightloper's mouth. He knows the nightloper won't kill a female as valuable as Beth is. But a nightloper can do much that is shy of true death.

Slade pushes off the head of the lion. Strings of his partial mane cling to Slade's talons as they pop free of the bony skull. He falls to the ground, and Slade hops to the nightloper Beth rides.

The nightloper jerks Beth's foot from his mouth, and she slashes at his throat with exacting precision.

It nicks his flesh, but it's not a mortal wound.

Slade plows through two more nightlopers.

"No!" he bellows, and the nightloper's eyes flick to Slade's as he stands over Beth.

Mute understanding flows between them.

Do not touch her!

The nightloper's rows of teeth gleam as he follows Beth to the ground. Her elbows slam against the forest's undergrowth. She drops one of her blades as she breaks her fall.

Beth searches for reflections, but none exist within night's embrace on One.

A rat nightloper falls on Slade's back, sinking its teeth into his shoulder. As he runs toward Beth, he tosses it off, a chunk of his flesh in its teeth.

So much for ignoring instinct.

Beth buries her blade in the nightloper's shoulder, and the wolf's mouth opens wide.

Beth strikes the nightloper's throat with her knuckles, rolling away.

The wolf lands on her back.

She screams, and her gaze meets Slade's. Beth's eyes are flat black discs of fear and determination. Slade's emotions swell from the proof of her courage, and that small seed of tenderness he harbors grows larger.

Slade mutters a curse. This female has the bravest heart of any he's ever known. And a nightloper bite will make things far worse for her.

Slade rushes the distance, and something grabs his feet. He falls, kicking backward, and hears a satisfying crunch.

Beth raises her forearms to protect her face. Slade springs to his feet then leaps the remaining distance. He misses.

Slade leans forward and grabs the leg of her pants. He pulls her to him with everything he has…just as the wolf clamps down on her leg.

Slade's momentum sets the nightloper's teeth more soundly, and Beth wails.

Slade releases her immediately. Heaving a mighty hiss of rage-fueled venom, he lands on the nightloper.

He falls on top of Beth, killing the nightloper above her. The breath whooshes out of her body, and Slade quickly rolls off the nightloper's body, prying its mouth off Beth's leg.

Beth sharply inhales. "Get me up!" she says, her eyes frantically searching for the rest of the group as she struggles to move the wolf's body.

Slade rolls the nightloper off her, covering her wound with his large palm.

Their eyes meet. Silence replaces the war-torn sounds of moments before.

"What? Slade—where is everyone?"

Slade says nothing but slides his arms underneath her and stands.

"I can walk, Slade."

Fine. He sets Beth on her feet, and she takes a step before slamming a hand into his arm. "Principle—what is it?"

"Poison."

Beth blinks as more nightlopers charge toward them.

Slade spots a rope dangling five feet away, and he makes a decision.

Beth's already crouched, poison dulling her eyes. Her limbs tremble as she readies for the next siege.

"Forgive me, tiny frog."

Slade picks her up by the armpits and heaves her at the rope. "Grab ahold!" he bellows as she flies.

Beth reaches for the rope, automatically twisting her small legs around its breadth.

His eyes hold hers for a heartbeat as she's hoisted toward the sky. Toward safety.

"Slade!" she screams.

He ignores her and turns to face his enemy.

19

Merrick

Merrick grabs for Beth, kicking himself for letting Slade protect her when, clearly, he wasn't up for the job.

She clutches at him, latching on to his fingers, and he easily swings her onto the platform.

"Jeb—" She turns so quickly, she almost loses her balance, and he tightens his hold.

"Get back," he grinds out and wraps an arm around her.

"We can't leave Slade down there!" she yells.

We most certainly can.

If only Jeb could be so fortunate for the hulking Bloodling to meet a timely end at the hands of the nightlopers.

He gently moves Beth from the edge and turns her.

The snarls, yips, and growls are not so easily ignored. Beth tries to look, and Jeb grasps her chin, forcing her to look at him. "Let Slade deal with his enemy, Beth. He risked his gray skin to save you."

"I know," she whispers. "I've been an ass. Ungrateful."

Jeb shakes his head. Something is going on under the surface here; Jeb can feel it—and it has nothing to do with her conduct. "Stay here. He'll work it out."

"Or not," Jacky says from behind Jeb.

Jeb whirls, keeping a hold on Beth, lest she careen over the slim rail and plummet right back into the pit of nightlopers.

"Hey, dude." Jacky backs away, hands raised.

Jeb seethes at him then looks behind Jacky. Kennet, Maddie, and Jacky are standing in a loose cluster while Gunnar speaks in low tones with some other Bloodlings.

"Where are the female Reflectives?" Jeb realizes he's absently stroking Beth's arm, and he forces himself to lower his hand, secure in the knowledge she's given up the idea of tossing herself back into the fray.

Gunnar breaks from his conversation. "The females have taken them for food and clothes. Calvin accompanies them."

"So they're not off getting a little fang blood draw?" Jacky asks suspiciously, putting his pointer fingers in his open mouth to dangle.

He has a point.

Howling raises the hackles of everyone in the tree home, and Gunnar shoots a dismissive glance below, where Jeb assumes Slade is fighting for his life.

They really do let their own fight. That would never work in the world of the Reflectives, where everything is about partners. Or—it *was.*

"The women are safe. We didn't come all this way to outrun your corrupt Reflectives, only to debase defenseless women. Do you know nothing of our traditions?"

Jeb doesn't.

A howl that sounds like sure death wails from below, and everyone crowds to the rail.

Slade is making his way up one of the many ropes, hand over powerful hand. Without appearing to breathe, he glides effortlessly up the vine-like strands.

He swings near the top, and his feet catch the lip of the wood platform. Slade heaves himself up to grab the rail with one hand, and he hooks the rope on top of a peg with the other. He jumps over the rail that hugs the platform's perimeter.

His eyes calm when they light on Beth.

Jeb wants to push him back into the mess below.

"How did you get away?" Slade looks to Gunnar. "Thank you for your assistance."

Gunnar's lips quirk at Slade's glare. "You did not need it."

Slade grunts and walks to Beth, who moves to meet him. The slap she delivers echoes in the intimate space beneath the low ceilings of the open tree house.

"Don't you ever do that again. I could have *helped*." She trembles with rage.

Slade grabs the hand that hit him, and Jeb strides forward. Slade presses his lips to Beth's open palm, meeting Jeb's eyes over the top of her fingertips.

Jeb growls, moving right into Slade's chest. Three inches separates them in height, but nothing does so in intellect or ingenuity.

"Don't touch her."

Slade's head cocks to the side, his eyebrow sweeping in a sardonic tilt. "She wants me to, hopper. Do you not feel her blood call to mine?"

Jeb doesn't even turn to look at Beth. He forecasts nothing. One minute, his hands are by his side; the next, his fist is buried in the Bloodling's gut.

Beth jerks out of the way.

Slade bends in half, taking the strike, and Jeb raises his knee, plowing his kneecap into the Bloodling's face. Slade begins to drop, jabbing Jeb between the legs so hard that Jeb falls to the floor, holding his nuts while blood from Slade's nose sprays them both.

"Boys!" Gunnar strides toward them as Beth backs away. "Play nice!"

"Jeb!" Beth yells.

Gunnar seizes Jeb's nape as well as Slade's bound hair and slams their heads together.

The sheer strength of the maneuver shocks Jeb even as he falls back, still clutching his balls, while stars explode in his narrowing vision.

"He can kick some *ass*," Jacky says in awestruck wonder from the sidelines.

Jeb would cheerfully kill Jacky if he could reach him. But he's too busy holding down his gorge.

"Now. Beth is safe, while you two infants play at being males. My daughter should not have to contend with the likes of you while being in danger."

Beth looks from Merrick to Slade. "Nobody's fighting over me. Jeb is my partner—Slade is a relative."

Jeb glances at Beth and doesn't like how pale she is.

Slade chokes, getting to his hands and knees on the floor, gurgling a response.

"What?" Gunnar asks, cupping his palm behind his ear. "I can't hear that."

"He said she's not his kin," Maddie answers in a hesitant voice.

Jeb sees the fear in her face as she looks at Gunnar.

Jeb's nausea rolls through him as he struggles to stand. Beth grabs his elbow, and pride makes him pull away from her. She retreats, giving him his space.

His crotch throbbing, Jeb glares down at Slade, who also manages to gain his footing.

Gunnar stands loosely between them. "Now that I have your attention, let's run through the facts."

Jeb says nothing, pleased that he's no longer in the fetal position.

"I have found I have a daughter, because by pure happenstance, I jumped with Slade." Gunnar's nearly black eyes look at each face in the room, including the two Bloodlings who hang back, staying out of the chaos. "We have brought back a few hoppers."

"Sounds like one of those bigotry names," Jacky says from his corner of the large room.

"This isn't the time for political correctness," Maddie comments softly.

"Uh-huh, whatever."

Gunnar's eyes narrow on Jacky. "If you mean that *hopper* is a derogatory term for a Reflective, then you are correct."

"Wasn't Beth's mom a hopper?" Jacky asks smoothly, keeping a smug grin on his face.

"She was," Gunnar answers without expression.

"Then why put down a whole species if you dug her so much, and—duh—there's your daughter." Jacky's palm swings toward Beth. "She hops pretty well, and so do you, big dude." Jacky's self-satisfied grin widens just a touch.

"All true. But I am pure Bloodling. It is an honor to jump if the blood of the hoppers doesn't flow in my veins."

Jacky snorts. "You guys are as stuck up as them." Jacky jerks his jaw toward Kennet and Jeb.

"Perhaps. But before my incarceration, I managed the Bloodlings under the steadfast hand of Gunnar's sire."

"What happened?" Beth asks, giving a nervous glance below.

Slade follows her gaze. "They won't climb to get to us."

Her eyes shift to Slade. "Why?"

"The vines are poisonous to nightloper blood."

"Awesome," Jacky deadpans.

Gunnar ignores the side conversation and returns to his history. "In any event, with the Bloodling king deceased and after my unfortunate breakdown and subsequent imprisonment, the slaver had easy access to our females."

Beth and Jeb step forward.

"It's been twenty years that Dimitri has held our women, keeping us in our place through threats of violence against them."

Maddie walks out to stand before Gunnar and Slade. "What did they do?"

Gunnar's eyes dip, and Slade speaks to the pockets of open forest, where branches move swiftly, beating against each other. The melody of the leaves churns its own music here on One.

Gunnar lifts his eyes and takes her chin gently, turning her face as if studying a prize. "Something that will never happen to you, little hopper."

She moves her face away from his hand. "It's Madeline."

He frowns, dropping his hand to his side.

"He looks like a guy that just got shut down, Maddie. Nice."

Maddie doesn't look at Jacky. "I'm not shutting anyone down. But we've established *hopper* is their crass name for Reflective."

Gunnar suddenly grips her shoulders and jerks her toward him. Maddie gives a startled yelp, and the two

Bloodling guards surge forward, barring the others from interfering.

"We shared blood, Madeline." Gunnar says her name strangely, like musical notes barely caressed.

"So?" she replies in a shaking voice.

He looks at the Reflectives. "Who understands any Bloodling history?"

Beth sighs. "I guess I should have stopped it." She looks down at her feet then stubbornly raises her chin. "But the truth is, even though I'm angry with your neglect of me—"

"Ignorance," Gunnar corrects.

Beth ignores him. "I couldn't let you die. I knew what would happen if Maddie gave you blood, and I wanted you to live worse than I cared about her fate. It was wrong. And selfish."

Beth turns to Maddie, and Jeb's gut tightens. Whatever she will say is not good.

Maddie swallows hard. "What does me giving him blood have to do with anything?"

Beth inhales deeply. "A blood donation from a kindred is similar to having sex."

"What?!" Jackie yells, slapping his forehead. "No way!"

Maddie takes a step backward, increasing her distance from Gunnar.

"Yes way," Beth replies, easily slipping into Three terminology.

Jeb shuts his eyes. *Another complication we didn't need.*

Perfect.

"How could you?" Maddie whirls, facing Beth. "I mean, I—" She flushes a deep red. "I haven't done that, with anyone."

"Huh?" Jacky scratches his head. "Not even Chase?"

Jeb groans as Maddie bursts into tears. "I didn't know. I just—I had to help him. It's like my body demanded it!"

Jeb folds his arms.

What a fucking mess.

"I'm sorry, Maddie. I can't take it back. And honestly, I want answers from him." Beth turns and glares at her father. "And by Principle, I will get them."

"In time, my hopper daughter, you shall know more than you ever wished to."

Jeb doesn't like the ominous ring to Gunnar's words, mainly because they sound like the truth.

And that has been in short supply since they met up with the Bloodlings.

20

Slade

Slade can feel the nightloper's hate, their lust to taste his blood, but the nightlopers no doubt took their orders from Dimitri.

He knew the escape was too easy, too choreographed. There were far too many nightlopers for the others to have remained unscathed, and for only him and Beth to be left on the ground.

But Slade was unwilling to give Beth up on their terms.

They would be in for a surprise.

Their unerring gazes travel after Beth as she's pulled high above them. Their expressions of just missing the prize would be comical if the situation weren't so grave.

Only when she is safely ensconced inside his home in the trees does he turn his attention to the lion nightloper.

His gold eyes flash in the heavy gloom and slowly spin. Caught as both animal and humanoid, the nightloper is forever between the two forms, destined for a nocturnal existence.

The lion bares his teeth, and a wolf nightloper behind him howls mournfully.

The lion steps forward, tossing a partial mane behind him. Cheekbones like slash marks hover beneath the piercing gaze of captured twin suns. A muffled roar as soft as a whisper slips between his lips, and talons click as he clenches his fist.

"You were to hand the hopper over."

"Yes." Slade nods. "I will. In my own way, at my own time."

The lion circles Slade, and Slade wags a finger in his direction. "Be of a care, before I take your head and feed on the rich blood from your neck."

A true roar issues forth, sending a raw echo floating above them.

The others will think I am being ripped to shreds. The deception would be fitting to cover his current bit of maneuvering.

"Dimitri tries to gain Beth Jasper before the remaining half of the females of our kind have been returned."

"What's left of them." A hyena nightloper snickers behind Slade.

Slade spins, slicing the hyena's throat with two talons. The hyena's speckled eyes widen; half-animal hands move to circle his throat. A long gash appears like a yawing second mouth.

The surrounding nightlopers observe but do not interfere.

When the wound fills with blood, they attack the hyena.

Slade watches with a detached amusement. In typical nightloper fashion, they consume the weak.

His attention returns to the lion. The yips and yelps of the feeding nightlopers create a terrible din. *Again, good cover for subterfuge.*

The lion heaves a great exhale. "I cannot kill you, Prince of the Bloodlings. I can only deliver the message. But know this"—he points an amber-colored talon at Slade's chest, and Slade folds his arms, feigning boredom when actually, he is cautious of the lion's movements—"Dimitri will be most unhappy you did not deliver the hopper."

Slade walks into the talon. It pierces his chest, and blood runs down his breastbone from the shallow wound. "There will be no hopper *mate* for Dimitri lest he agree to the rightful exchange agreed upon. She for our females. That is all."

Slade steps back and opens his arms in mock surrender.

Then he shows the lion his back in a fluid spin and leap, easily grabbing the hanging rope that would blacken nightloper fingers from touch alone.

He climbs with steady sure arms, one after the other, as he has done for three centuries.

Dimitri will not have Beth Jasper, nor will Jeb Merrick.

She is his alone.

And the females belong to no one but the Bloodlings.

Slade does not think he can't have it all. He was born to rule.

And rule he shall.

"You're still bleeding," Beth tells Slade as they gather with the others around a table within the five connected tree homes of Bloodling royalty.

Many more curious eyes study the Reflectives from afar, hidden by vine and tree. Slade can feel their eyes on the group, and he wonders if the foreigners do, as well.

Slade dabs at the superficial wound. "Nightloper damage heals more slowly," he says, giving a shrug of both dismissal and explanation.

Jeb glares at Slade from across the table, and Slade smirks, enjoying the discomfort of his competition for Beth's affections.

The Reflective male is a creature of high self-importance. Beth, who is seated beside Slade, seems to have missed that abject lesson of arrogance so prolific within believers of The Cause.

Slade realizes his thought process is somewhat unfair. Jeb is a highly skilled fighter—all hoppers are. After all, Lance Ryan almost killed him in that ring. If it hadn't been for Slade's superior healing ability, Reflective Ryan might have been the victor.

Slade belches quietly behind his fist, searching for the servant nightloper to signal for more blood. Sloth nightlopers, one of the few nightloper breeds who can stand the life in the trees, are the natural slaves of the Bloodlings. One sees him and comes forward.

Maddie shies away from the sloth. His stealthy movements and glowing eyes might be too new for the frail Three.

"Do not be afraid. They're harmless," Gunnar says, frowning in concern.

Jacky throws up his hands. "Okay. I'd die for some fries." He looks around the table, picking up some greens for the first course and letting them fall with a finger flick. "That aside, I'd like to mention how freaking weird it is that you guys have rodents serving you up in a tree house with half-animal dudes circling the trees down below. Sorry, there's just no way to explain the weird out of that. So Maddie being kinda blown away by the bizarre bullshit of—where the hell are we?"

Beth lets her chin collapse into her fist with apparent resignation. "One."

Jacky snaps his fingers. "*Right*—One. Is just the tip of the weirdness iceberg. So, yeah, she's kind of afraid of all the new sights in this place. And I can't say I'm all on board, either. And can we get some real food? I know you dudes aren't surviving on this." He points at the greens.

"That *is* food," Slade comments in a dry voice.

He and Gunnar share a glance, then his eyes turn to Jacky. "I think, while you're here, if you don't want to be in a sequestered location *alone* you will censor your commentary, Three."

Jacky sighs. "And everyone's so butt hurt all the time."

"Jacky," Maddie says in a warning tone.

"Tell me I'm lying?" he asks her.

Maddie shakes her head, biting her lip. "Not lying," she agrees softly, a smile softening her mouth.

Gunnar's eyebrow slowly rises, and she gives him a nervous glance.

"But," she adds, "we're their guests. We're at their mercy. The Reflectives are kinda crazy, and those *things* are down there. This is as good as it's going to get."

Jacky seems to ponder her words. "Okay, but first chance we get, we're popping back to Earth, and I'm eating about ten pizzas and ordering a case of amnesia that lasts"—Jacky's eyes go to the thatched roof—"about since the day my ass landed in Papilio."

"You're an ungrateful prick," Merrick says in a steady voice.

Slade leans back, putting his arm around Beth and cupping her shoulder.

Merrick's face darkens as Beth gives Slade a speculative look.

"Yup. Stick a fork in me; I'm done." The Three doesn't even bother to defend his conduct.

Slade likes that. "Let the crazed hoppers come."

Jacky turns his attention to Slade—they all do.

"It will not matter. We are the species with the brains."

"What about the night guys?" Jacky asks.

"There are more of them than us," Slade admits neutrally.

"So they can't puzzle shit out, but there's a lot of them, and they go hard."

Slade blinks, rapidly wading through Jacky's strange terminology. "Yes."

"Then it's not bad that you have some Reflectives and me here." He jabs a thumb in his chest.

Slade's eyebrows rise. "Oh?" The young Three will grow into his manhood, but he is short and not fully muscled yet. Of course, Three males are not renowned for their physiques.

Jacky nods, ignoring Slade's slow perusal. "Yup. You see, I don't care about politics, hurting people's feelings, or taking long showers together. I want to get *home*. I want Maddie to come with." His eyes meet the others' stares. "And Merrick's got a permanent stick embedded in his ass."

Merrick rises.

Jacky's eyes fly to him. "Chill! God, Merrick." His gaze shifts back to Slade. "But he does the right thing."

"He has integrity," Maddie adds.

"Exactly," Jacky says, giving her a smile. He laces his hands behind his head and grins across the table. "And Jasper, well, she's in a tight spot, but she's got an assload of dudes running around, trying to protect her."

Beth's chin comes off her fist, and she opens her mouth.

Jacky rolls his eyes. "Not that she's down with that."

She closes her mouth then opens it again. "Absolutely not. I don't need a male to protect me."

Merrick looks at her.

Slade does, as well.

Color sweeps her cheekbones. "Usually," she amends with barely veiled embarrassment.

"What I'm saying is, I'm a pain in the ass, but I'll get the job done. Because I'm motivated."

"To return to that criminal planet. Three?" Gunnar confirms.

"You got it. Criminal or not, there's not a bunch of vamps and night-whatevers waiting to knock you on your ass and suck you dry." He slaps his thighs, and Maddie jumps.

"Okay. Said my piece." He looks down at the wilting greens.

"Got any meat in this joint?"

Slade grins. He likes the boy very much.

He'll be a perfect sacrifice if the situation presents.

And most certainly, one will.

21

Beth

"May I speak with you?" Jeb asks, and Beth struggles to keep her relief from washing over her face. She's pleased to have a safe place to have five seconds to communicate with Jeb in private.

But Beth worries Slade's tree houses might somehow be just another prison.

She longs for Papilio, the vineyards outside her windows, and her butterflies. Sadness beats at her insides, and a lump of unshed tears clogs her throat.

She fights her feelings, shoving them deep inside.

Jeb reaches for her arm.

Beth visualizes Slade's dark eyes gazing up at her from the forest floor as nightlopers surround him.

He was calm; Beth is not.

"Beth?" Jeb shakes her gently.

His hand circles her upper arm, and she chokes back a sob as those stuffed emotions well to the surface again.

"Don't touch me—I can't handle it, Jeb. I miss my home, our life…The Cause."

In the semi-privacy of his small borrowed tree room he pulls her against him.

She hits his chest with her fist. "Don't," she repeats.

Jeb murmurs reassurances into her ear, closing his massive hand around her small one. "It's okay, Beth. I'm here."

Beth rests her forehead between the flat muscular planes of his chest. His heart beats against her temple.

"It's all right to be sad. Give yourself permission to be female, Beth. It's not a sin."

His warm hands fall to her middle back, caressing at the same time they draw her nearer into the strength of his body.

Beth groans in defeat. The feel of Jeb's arms around her and the comfort he offers her is irresistible when she's so emotionally fragile. Beth has lived in abject loneliness for too long, with only the blessing of the Principle, her brains, and an inherent reflective ability to aid her.

Her hands are free, and it's bad.

But it feels so good. Her fingertips inch their way around Jeb's trim waist and sink into the hollow at the small of his back, mirroring his hold on her.

"Beth," he squeezes out between clenched teeth, "I can't hold back with my soul mate. You're playing with fire."

She tips her head back, and Jeb's pale-gray eyes have darkened threateningly. "You would hurt me?"

He gives the barest shake of his head, drawing a finger along her cheekbone, then cups the side of her face. "Never."

"Then I have nothing to worry about. If I have to back away, would you allow it?"

Jeb's lips curl, and he says tenderly, "I would not like it, Reflective Jasper."

Her face falls, and she bites her lip, tears threatening.

"Hey now." Jeb bends down and tilts her chin up so that he can look deep into her eyes. "I meant that as a compliment. I don't see you as I do other females. You are a Reflective warrior—I haven't forgotten."

"*And* your soul mate?" she asks, searching his eyes, still in disbelief.

"Always that. Never doubt it." His hand glides to her nape, and Beth's eyes close. She sinks into the gentle touch of his murderous hands, hands like her own.

"I'm sure that will bring you nothing but grief on Papilio," a sarcastic voice says from behind them.

Beth gasps, and Jeb puts her protectively behind him.

Slade's huge bulk fills the doorway.

Beth hears the dry click as she swallows. "Try knocking." Her voice sounds like a toad's song.

Slade's hand slowly rises, and with great exaggeration, he raps loudly twice on the wooden threshold. Beth fold's her arms, glaring at him in irritation.

Slade saved her, and Beth has to admit, she feels something for him. She's not sure what—a sense of kinship or possibly gratefulness for saving her from Ryan? *More?*

But right now, he's pushing all of her buttons.

"What rancor or problems come about from my declaration should not concern a Bloodling," Jeb says, and Beth winces at his tone.

He says Bloodling as if he means to say *imbecile.*

Slade hears the disrespect as clearly as Beth does, and he strides forward.

Jeb moves her aside.

"No, Jeb," Beth says quickly.

She feels a little bad about what she does next. In a flash, she slashes her forearm with her own ceramic blade—deeper than she intended.

Beth cringes as a line of red appears on an arm already littered with the fine scars reminiscent of her profession. *What's one more?*

Slade halts, his head jerking to the wound, nostrils flaring at the scent of her blood. "What have you done?" he roars at her, fangs lengthening.

"What I had to." Her voice resonates in the space.

"Dammit, Beth!" Jeb grabs her wrist, and Slade's hand is suddenly there, as well, gripping the arm that holds hers.

The two males pull against each other as Beth bleeds. She knows what she must do, and she doesn't like it. But some evils are necessary.

"I'm hurt," she says in a voice full of something she never calls upon—feminine wiles.

Slade drops Jeb's arm as though burnt and picks up her wounded one. His eyes dilate, and his fangs extend to their full length.

His breathing is erratic, and his black gaze swells in her vision. It's all she can see, and she is all he stares at.

"Get your fucking fangs put away, Bloodling," Jeb says ominously.

"No, Jeb. Slade must heal me." Beth's eyes go to Slade's.

His lips part, and his pupils dilate, giving way to eyes like solid obsidian gems.

"Yes." He pulls her forward and runs his nose over her bleeding forearm, hovering just above the wound. His tongue snakes out, lapping the blood, and he groans. Jeb is forgotten, just as Beth knew he would be.

Slade leans his powerful body over hers and draws her closer with one arm.

Jeb inserts himself between them. "Beth—*no*. There must be another way."

"Take my blood, Slade. I invite you to partake of my vein."

Beth feels the pierce of his fangs, and Jeb seizes Beth around the waist, tense and ready to jerk her away from the feeding Bloodling.

"He'll tear my arm off," Beth says in a panicked voice.

Jeb's forehead flops against her shoulder, and he asks, "Why?"

"Because we need him. We need Slade to navigate the treacherous waters of One. I can't have you two at each other's throats and hope to survive this."

Slade devours her blood, and she begins to feel weak. A riot of goosebumps rise in response to his suckling, and deep inside Beth, an erotic response echoes with each pull of his mouth. Beth seizes a harsh breath.

Slade's eyes roll up to meet hers.

He knows.

Beth squeezes back her fear and surprise over her instant arousal, but the pulse between her legs frightens her more than anything in her entire life has. "We will own him a little with this," she breathes through harsh pants.

Jeb's arms squeeze around her. "Tell him to stop, or I'll kill him," he says with menace.

Beth hand reaches out, letting it hover reluctantly over the Bloodlings' inky hair. "Slade, stop. You're making me weak."

Immediately, the pulls become gentle, and the horrible flood of heat between her legs and the tingling of her breasts ease. The invisible thread of his sensual heat loosens. A shaky breath escapes her, and she sags where she stands.

Slade laps slowly, closing the wound.

Beth's eyes go round.

She can't see even a scar.

Yet the crimson proof of his consumption paints his lips ruby.

He bows at her feet, wrapping his huge arms around her thighs while Jeb hangs on to her waist.

"Thank you for the gift of your blood, tiny frog." His breath is hot just above and between her knees.

Beth opens her mouth to reply with actual coherent words, but she can't. A powerful feeling builds from within her, rushing from every part of her body. The residual arousal rears its head again, swamping her body with heat. A wave of pleasure surges inside her. The most feminine part of her clenches and releases in rhythmic pulses then explodes as she gives a hoarse cry, slipping in Jeb's arms.

He rights her. "Beth!"

She floats, horribly ashamed of everything. She knew of the history of blood sharing. If a female willingly gives blood to a male Bloodling, the donor has a measure of control. She wants that power over Slade while she is on One. *No more in-house fighting. It's about surviving the now then getting back to Papilio.*

Unfortunately, her history lessons failed to mention what would happen to the female while the male Bloodling fed.

Beth had just experienced her first orgasm in front of the man who declared her as his soul mate.

And he was not the male to cause that sensation.

Beth wrenches out of both their holds. Shame floods her face with fire, threatening to melt her skin. She stumbles and grabs the doorframe. The males call out to her, but she doesn't turn.

If she never faces either one of them again, that will be too soon.

Worse, Beth is sure that both males have heard their share of females in the throes of ecstasy.

Without looking back, she runs.

Jeb calls out again, but Slade remains silent. Beth knows he understands what his feed entailed, and he's probably laughing at her.

She runs, leaping between the homes without regard to the height or the nightlopers that might be below, until she's ten houses away. The shivering emerald canopy of trees is her only audience.

When Beth finds a platform high up and away from everything, she cradles her head in her arms and cries.

Her tears are for more than her current embarrassment, but also for the shame of being half-Bloodling herself. She mourns the mother who would hide her true ancestry and regrets that her father never knew of her birth or terrible upbringing. She cries for the two Threes she and Jeb stole away to her planet only to condemn them to danger. She weeps for the female Reflectives who might be jumping as she sits there, feeling sorry for herself. They might be jumping to Principle knows where, without locators, safety, or currency.

Beth cries until exhaustion overtakes her.

Gunnar

Gunnar jumps in silence, landing lightly onto the platform where Beth sleeps, tears staining her face.

The wood shifts and creaks underneath his weight.

His throat constricts when he sees how much this small hopper reminds him of Lucinda.

He watched Lucinda sleep many times. Gunnar's heart grows heavy as he observes his Reflective daughter in slumber.

He failed to protect her mother.

But he vows that will not be the case with Beth Jasper. Gunnar would die before he allows harm to befall her.

He scoops Beth up, cradling her against his chest. She's as light as a feather.

She fists his shirt in her sleep, uttering a quiet whimper. She wiggles closer, and his heart twists as a rare surge of tenderness overtakes him.

She feels right in his arms. Gunnar wants to take her somewhere safe. His life will have been worth living if he can just see that one thing through.

And Dimitri must never know of her.

Gunnar will discuss with Slade about keeping Beth's presence secret. The nightlopers have already seen the foreigners.

If word gets back to Dimitri, it will be bad for them all. As far as Dimitri is concerned, Beth is just a hopper.

If he knew she shares Bloodling genetics, Dimitri would exploit that rare combination.

Nightlopers have few females.

Dimitri would surely want Beth for himself. As long as he is alive, Dimitri will not have her.

With Beth still in his arms, he turns and leaps off the platform then catches the next platform with expert footing.

Gunnar makes his way back to where Beth's temporary room is, but his eyes scan the forest floor.

Worry is his companion all the way back.

22

Merrick

"You are a colossal pain in the ass."

"I'm aware." Jacky leans back, lacing his fingers behind his head and trying to get comfortable on the strangest couch Jeb's ever seen.

Why bother sitting down when it's practically at floor level?

"Now you're just repeating yourself, Merrick."

The Three is right. If Jeb were not in the throes of being soul mated, he could think and react better. Now all the focus of working under The Cause has shifted to Beth.

Beth.

Jeb pinches the bridge of his nose.

"Hit a nerve, bud?"

Jeb's eyes snap open. "If you don't prove useful in the next five seconds, I'm throwing you over the rail."

Jacky's eyebrows pop, and he glowers.

"Fine." He leans forward to rest his forearms on his knees, letting his hands dangle between them. "I don't trust the Bloodlings."

Jeb's lips thin. He doesn't, either. "Agreed."

"The big dude is crushing on Beth, and I know you've 'declared' her or whatever—so all the more reason to get out of here and fast."

Jeb rocks back on his heels, folding his arms. "I understand all this. What is your point? You came along because we had no choice in the matter." What Jeb didn't say was how much he wanted to do a jump to Three and return Jacky and Maddie to where they belonged. They would absolutely be safer on Three than on One. But traveling to One was a necessary detour because of the volatility on Papilio.

"Love your delivery, Merrick."

Jeb's gaze hardens like a diamond on Jacky. "I'm not a soft man, Jacky. And for that, I apologize."

Jacky raises his hand. "No problem. But I'm not a soft guy, either. I've been through some shit—Maddie even more. All I'm saying is—I feel responsible for her. I want to get back to earth. I know *that* place. Sure, there's paranormals, but we don't have night-whatevers, and we sure as hell don't have vamps."

Jeb doesn't contradict him on that last misinformation, but it's a challenge not to offer clarity. Knowledge makes the tip of his tongue tingle.

"Now Maddie's given blood to freaky Gunnar, who is somehow Beth's dad." He flings his bangs out of his face, and Jeb is suddenly struck by how ancient his eyes look for one so young. "I just see us getting sucked into this weirdness and don't want to. Promise me you'll get us back to that lake were you can jump us back to earth."

"Reflectives do not give their word lightly."

Jacky's lips turn up. "I know. Why do you think I'm askin'?"

Jeb sighs in frustration. "I will do my utmost."

"You trust Kennet and Calvin?" he asks.

Jeb jerks his chin back. "Yes. Why?"

"We might need them."

"Jacky, Reflective Jasper, Kennet, Calvin, and I *must* return to Papilio. It is where our destiny lies. Even now, though many might have sought Beth—" Jeb takes two deep breaths to quell his anger. "Order *will* be restored. We will find Rachett. If we can't, then a new hierarchy will be established so The Cause will not be interrupted any further than it already has been." He pauses for a moment. "Thirteenth: *Forsake not The Cause*," Jeb recites more to himself than for Jacky's benefit.

"Yeah, okay." Jacky heaves his eyes upward. "So you get us to earth *before* you go back to Papilio and go all cosmic on the sectors again."

Jeb works through Jacky's slang quickly. "Yes."

"Deal?" Jacky asks, his eyes on Jeb's like a hawk's.

"Yes," he repeats.

A knock lands with a hollow echo at the door. "Come," Jeb says.

Gunnar walks through. "I've found her."

Jeb moves forward. "I sensed she wasn't in danger…"

Gunnar flicks his hand in dismissal. "She needed time away from the males."

Jeb's face flames. He did not endanger his soul mate, though that seems to be what her father implies.

"Her response to Slade is…" He clears his throat delicately. "Natural in a Bloodling female." His lips twitch. "Though it may have taken our Beth by surprise."

Jeb's blood rushes hotter, though it makes him feel slightly better that Gunnar seems as offended as he is.

That fucking Bloodling gave Beth an orgasm. He is certain that she would not have volunteered her blood so readily had she understood the outcome.

And Slade had Principledamned known it, the smug bastard.

Gunnar watches Jeb's face, and he clamps down on his impulses with an effort.

Jeb wants to be the male to pleasure Beth—if she ever affords him the opportunity. Slade violated her, but Jeb is sure the Blooding doesn't see it that way. Slade takes. That's all he's good for.

Jeb deliberately steers the conversation away from the awkward discussion of Beth's sexuality and toward something that will get them back to Papilio. Why Gunnar seems to be so matter-of-fact about delicate discussion escapes Jeb. It must be a Bloodling trait. Still, his face had been tight as he said it.

The sooner they return and establish order, the better.

"She will awake on her own in a few hours. Giving of blood is tiring for a female, and she must take time to replenish her stores. I am sure Slade appreciates her gift."

Jeb's eyes lock with his.

Interesting. Those black eyes glitter with anger, confirming Jeb's suspicion of Gunnar's discontent. *So Daddy Dearest isn't happy Slade took Beth's blood, either.* Perhaps Slade committed some kind of social *faux pas.*

Gunnar suddenly straightens, wiping unease from his face. "Slade will make recompense. As any decent male Bloodling should."

Jacky looks between the two of them, missing nothing.

That's just what Jeb needs, a thousand questions from the inquisitive Three.

"A sloth will come and get you when Beth awakes."

Jeb gives a curt nod in both thanks and salutation, but the great Bloodling lingers, his light-gray skin shimmering slightly in the fading light of the day, though direct sunlight doesn't pierce the dense canopy of trees.

Jacky's eyebrows slowly rise.

Jeb waits.

"I have a question of you, Jeb Merrick."

Clearly. "Speak, Gunnar of the Bloodlings," Jeb replies formally.

"I-I inquire after the young *hop*—Three."

Jeb stands in stunned silence.

Jacky jumps up like he's on fire. "*Maddie?*"

Gunnar reluctantly gives Jacky his attention. "Yes. Madeline."

"Why? 'Cause you're into her?"

Jeb's brows come together, and his loosely folded arms fall to his sides. He quickly glances at Jacky, whose eyes say so much. Jeb is a believer in clarity. "Is this true?" Jeb asks Gunnar, his mind has been consumed with other things, "Do you wish for something between you and Madeline? Because she is technically a Reflective… though she is from Three."

"She's kinda young for you, ya old pervert." Jacky plants his feet wide, challenging the dangerous Bloodling with his stance and his unflinching stare.

"Technically, Bloodlings age very slowly. I am nearing thirty of your earth years. We only age ten years for every one hundred of yours on Three."

"What?" Jacky asks in a choked voice. "So you're like three *hundred*?"

"Or so…" Gunnar replies in a bored tone, waffling his palm.

"Okay." Jacky sounds sick.

"I will determine this, Jacky," Jeb says

He winks, and just like that, he hands the verbal reins to Jeb, who is profoundly grateful.

"What interest do you have in the girl?" Jeb asks.

"So any claim I might have for the girl is void because you don't have enough females in your world?" Gunnar heaves a disgusted exhale. "That is a weak excuse. *No* sector has adequate women, aside from Three and maybe two others. I have as much right as the next. But I endeavored to ask after her family. Perhaps if her sire was to meet with me…"

He let the sentence hang there.

"There's no dad." Jacky glances at Jeb, and Jeb favors him with a frown of warning, which the Three promptly ignores. "In fact, Jeb and Beth went back and did old Chuck in."

"'Old Chuck'?" Gunnar puts his hands on his hips.

"Yeah. Reflectives don't mess around, Gunnar. Chuck was beating the hell out of Maddie and her mom, so when Jeb and Beth went back, he got what was coming to him."

Gunnar swings his face to Jeb, regarding him. "I thank you for that, Merrick."

Jeb hangs his head, embarrassed that Reflective business is being bandied about for everyone to hear. *Principle.*

Yet he meets Gunnar's ominous stare with the truth. "It was my pleasure."

Gunnar nods. "So there is *no* family to impede my courtship."

"No, not in the classical sense, but the timing—" Jeb throws up his hands. "And as far as we know, she has no Bloodling heritage."

A faint smile hovers over Gunnar's lips. "Though her blood calls to me, Merrick."

"That kindred blood crap?" Jacky asks.

Gunnar stares at Jacky until the Three's eyes fall.

"It is not 'crap,' but a rare marker of compatibility. Beth's mother has been gone almost two decades."

"Did you have this kindred thing with her?" Jacky asks.

He's so far out of turn, Jeb doesn't even know where to begin.

"Yes," Gunnar answers, his chin hiking slightly. "That time with Lucinda was the happiest I've ever been."

Jacky snorts. "Listen, good for you. But Maddie might say, 'Thanks but no thanks.' What then? Last I heard, she likes the idea of getting the hell out of here and getting back to earth. Doing you a good turn on a little blood bank won't change that."

Gunnar is silent for a full minute.

When he speaks, it's with absolute conviction. "I believe I can make her an offer she cannot refuse."

Jeb would like very much to know what that is, but Gunnar gives him a nod and leaves before he can ask.

After a tense silence, Jacky says, "I think we have bigger fish to fry than the Reflectives chasing our tails."

Jeb can only nod his agreement.

23

Slade

Slade leans against the window frame outside Beth's borrowed loft. He stares into the far distance, where the forest meets the desert. The wide, hot plains of sand are the only buffer between the Bloodlings and Dimitri's fortress.

Slade exhales in frustration. He's purposefully placed Beth in the most defensible place. With a lesser female—a weaker one—it would not be as critical. A weaker female would have no means of defense if the male Bloodlings were to fall to invasion. The females would be helpless against the inevitable nightloper onslaught.

But not Beth Jasper.

Beth does have means, resourceful ones.

Slade steps away from his study of the great forest and turns that scrutiny to Beth. His eyes trace each line of her delicate face, marveling at the violent skill set contained within such a fragile-looking package.

His tiny frog can jump, fight—and respond. Slade's tongue darts out, wetting lips gone suddenly dry from the memory of their blood share.

Slade allows himself the fantasy of killing Dimitri. And therein lies the problem. It *is* fantasy. The nightlopers outnumber the Bloodlings three to one.

Everyone knows that Bloodlings are first species to originate on One. Just because the nightlopers' numbers are higher, that fact is not indicative of superiority.

Interspecies mating is rare, though Slade is sure, judging by the broken females who were returned, that the nightlopers tried.

In ancient times, vampires and Singers had shapeshifting abilities. If a nightloper had a small amount of lineage belonging to one or the other, a throwback offspring could occur between a nightloper and Bloodling—if the female could survive the mating.

Slade represses a shudder and completely misses Merrick's approach until the Reflective is almost upon him.

Slade whirls, and Merrick tenses. There is no love lost between them. They are both aware of the other's feelings for tiny frog, sleeping most gently inside a room of Slade's choosing.

"She still sleeps?" Merrick inquires softly.

Slade nods.

Their mutual postures relax, and Merrick motions for Slade to step away from the window. Though he wants to, Slade doesn't cast a last glance at Beth. Merrick already ascertains more of his true feelings than he would like.

Merrick drops silently to the lower platform, then Slade swings his arm to a vine and slides down behind him.

"What?" Slade asks.

"Do you know of our soul mate history?" Merrick asks.

Slade does.

However, he doesn't care. If Merrick is in the throes of heart-sickening agony because he has claimed Beth, it's of no concern to Slade.

He has a world of responsibility on his shoulders. His sire is gone, and his father's former first is unstable, while Beth's natural father is sniffing around a female from another sector.

Bloodlings are not at their best once their sights are pinned on a potential mate.

Gunnar has unexpectedly become a potential problem.

Only Slade can save the remaining Bloodling females, and the biggest consideration is his growing and undeniable feelings for Beth Jasper.

His task would be much simpler if he could just hand her over to Dimitri, reacquire the Bloodling females, and dust off his hands of their acquaintance.

But a mating with Dimitri would break Beth.

Though he is a nightloper of mixed origin, his sheer physicality might kill her.

Slade can't stand the idea of another male's hands touching Beth. That realization was the first nail in the coffin of his heart.

He remembers when she dragged herself out of the lake that fateful day, the huge Reflective sprinting after her. She was like a small drenched mouse escaping a cat.

His smile dissolves as he contemplates how quickly that changed when she ran into him.

Beth would have bounced off him and into the arms of Lance Ryan. But in that moment, Slade felt the call of more than just kindred blood. As much as Jeb Merrick believed Beth to be his other half, Slade knows there could be more than one half in the sectors that fit perfectly with another.

And right now, Beth is Slade's missing piece. Slade is certain, especially after what transpired during her gift of blood. No other female makes his blood hum with a melody only he can hear.

His brows lower over his eyes as he studies Merrick. Slade has to admit Merrick is the finest example of a Reflective he's ever seen. At first glance, he seems little more than an oversized Three.

But Reflectives are notoriously dangerous. Fast and terribly strong, they're trained to kill and jump. Not always in that order.

Jeb Merrick might be a few inches shorter than Slade is, but every inch of him is hard-won killer. Slade doesn't forget.

"Yes," he finally answers Merrick's question. "I know enough of your history to understand that your declaration doesn't matter to the tiny frog."

Merrick grimaces, crossing his arms, and Slade wonders what would happen if he just shoved Merrick over the rail.

Beth will hate me, he decides.

"Go ahead, Bloodling, shove me over the side."

Slade stifles a chuckle. *It's that obvious?* "Don't tempt me."

They stare at each other until Merrick finally gets to the point. "I plan to depart here. I thank you for your… hospitality—"

Merrick's choice of words makes Slade laugh.

He continues, "However, I intend to take the Threes to their home world first, then circle back around to Papilio. In our absence, I am certain Calvin can restore enough order for us to return. And"—Merrick's eyes meet Slade's—"I am also certain that many of our females were flung there." Merrick's face twists in obvious disgust. "If Beth and Kennet were to accompany me to Three, we could jump them back to Papilio and the male Reflectives' anxiety would cool. Right now, they have survived the last five years of a salacious rule. But no more."

Slade is silent, watching what must pass for passion with Merrick as he makes a sharp slicing gesture across his own throat.

Slade's lips curl as the motion gives him ideas better left unthought.

"Ryan is on the run, Rachett will be found, and order shall be restored."

Slade blanks his expression. He knows where Rachett is. He doesn't think Rachett will ever be fit for leadership again, though.

Merrick's face grows tight and wary as he scrutinizes Slade's expression. "What is it?"

Slade looks out into the dense leaves of the trees, where the breeze whistles between the tight spaces of the thick foliage. *It is now or never.* Merrick has unwittingly advanced Slade's motives.

"The slaver has Rachett."

Merrick's lips part in an almost-sigh. "Why did you not tell me straight away."

Slade balks at Merrick's accusation. "Because, believe it or not, there are politics here on One that take precedence over the mess of Papilio, Reflective Merrick."

Merrick steps in close to Slade's chest. The two of them stand, balanced precariously from the want of beating each other until their blood drips to the circling nightlopers below.

"Nothing," Merrick grates, "is more important that The Cause. You're foolish if you believe that the equilibrium of the sectors can tolerate any more disruption than they've already suffered at Ryan's misguided hand."

A thump behind them has them spinning on the landing platform.

Beth stands before them, her black eyes glittering, her cheeks rosy from sleeping.

Slade is struck by her beauty, and a pang of desire washes viciously inside him. He swallows the sensation.

"What's this about Rachett?" Her dark eyes assess Slade with something akin to distrust. The eyes she turns upon Merrick are filled with her feelings for him—trust, deference, and maybe more.

Slade clenches his fists, his talons pulsing for release.

She might not have claimed Merrick because she is unable to until the "timepiece" of their kind has halted its ticking, but there is *something* there.

Slade would give much to win such favor from her gaze.

As it is, she is unaware of her status as kindred to him. Still, the gift of her blood to him and his ability to give her pleasure could mean only one thing.

He is her kindred blood, as well.

Slade tosses a frozen smile on his face that's so stiff, it makes his face ache.

"Dimitri has Rachett."

Beth rushes to Merrick's side, and Slade's false smile slips a notch.

"Why are we standing here like idiots? We go get him. We can jump him back to Papilio, and things will be back to the way we were. Ryan had his chance to overthrow and implement his demented chaos. It's time to reassert The Cause." Beth looks between them.

Slade grinds his teeth. He can't allow Beth within five miles of Dimitri. However, he *can* get rid of two birds with one stone, as the Threes say.

"Merrick and I will rescue Rachett."

Beth's face glows with anger. "Do *not* demoralize my gender by assuming I will bow out of a reconnaissance mission, or that I might be intimidated by inevitable conflict."

Merrick and Slade exchange a look of understanding.

Merrick doesn't want Beth endangered any more that I. And he doesn't seem surprised that Slade volunteered him.

"Don't look at him like that," Beth says, punching Slade's arm. Her blow hurts, despite how small she is.

Slade jerks her away from Merrick, and his hand falls on Slade's arm.

"Worry not, hopper." Slade's eyes flick to Merrick, and his hand reluctantly withdraws. "I would never hurt our Beth."

A strange expression shadows Merrick's face momentarily, then it's gone.

"It is unsafe for any female to travel to Dimitri. Especially you. Do you so quickly forget the fun of Dimitri's holdings?"

He can see by the tension in her face that she remembers just fine.

"I'm not afraid, Slade."

Slade manages a completely genuine smile, his eyes moving over every contour of her face. "I know," he says softly, his grip becoming weaker, but shy of the caress he would like to give.

"In this, let us protect you." It kills Slade to make any concession to Merrick, but Slade will do it to see his agenda through.

Merrick gives him a glance full of speculative mistrust.

Slade hates his instincts. They're formidable.

Merrick jerks his head toward Slade. "He's right. Stay here with Maddie and Jacky. We'll return with Rachett."

No you won't, hopper.

Beth is silent for so long, Slade is sure her stubbornness will be the victor, but she surprises him.

She grips them both, and her voluntary touch causes Slade's emotions to mute his vocal chords.

"Come back to me then. Both of you." Her small hands are warm on his upper arm.

He fights every instinct he has to take her and crush her to him, protecting her body and soul from all who would hurt her. Instead, he does nothing. Only one of them will return.

Slade hates that Beth's regard includes Merrick.

But when he looks into her liquid eyes, he is bolstered that it also embraces him.

24

Beth

Something is going on.

Both Slade and Merrick are being cagey, and that deepens Beth's sensation of the portent of doom she's been living under recently.

She watches the two of them ready themselves to make the trek to Dimitri's fortress.

I wonder what or who he slaves now that he's lost the Reflectives?

Beth vividly remembers Dimitri's hands gripping her while his golden eyes spun slowly, piercing her. Beth's fight to remain calm and stoic in the face of a creature half-man, half-lion had been a fierce one.

Beth wanted to go fight alongside her partner simply because she's *afraid* to. Fear can't rule her. But Jeb and Slade had nearly begged her to stay. And she has Jacky and Maddie to consider. Yes, Kennet affords some protection, but...Maddie is too fragile for yet another person to abandon her. And ultimately, Beth and Jeb are responsible for the Threes.

Beth scans the landing platforms and houses, held and pierced by thick, ancient branches.

She gives a mournful exhale.

She's half-Bloodling and half-Reflective.

And wholly confused.

The Cause remains the most important thing in her life, but the men press in at all sides, making it hard for Beth to concentrate. She needs to return to Papilio. Word has been sent that Calvin, escorted by two Bloodlings, made the jump back to Ten. Even now, he should be restoring order in Papilio. Beth, Kennet, and Jeb need to find all the Reflective females and help with their healing—both physically and mentally. That should be her top priority—not this crazy game of Slade and Jeb battling for her affections.

If I knew how I felt, it'd be simple.

She forces her mind off the men and back to the important tasks. Whatever Reflectives who were in league with Ryan will be held accountable for their actions—if they have not already been justly murdered. The Reflectives who chased Beth as though they couldn't bear to have their last female out of sight will be reinstated into The Cause and will forget all about Beth upon the return of their females.

That is, unless her timepiece runs out and she find that Jeb is her soul mate—she would be unforgettable then.

Could I be that fortunate? Could it all be as simple as that? And what if I don't want to be anyone's soul mate? Maybe being a warrior of The Cause is a higher calling. She has at least one term left, and her timepiece is still fresh and ticking.

A horrible idea eats at the edges of her brain. What if her timepiece runs out and she finds she belongs with someone other than Jeb Merrick?

Slade, her mind whispers. Beth stiffens, heat suffusing her skin at just the memory of her orgasm. Beth is helpless to stop herself from imagining sex with the giant Bloodling. Her palms cover her cheeks, feeling the burning heat of her internal fantasy. She's a virgin, but she's not stupid. Beth could have given herself to any man in Papilio, because no Reflective would have her. None except Ryan. But his quest had all been about degrading her, rather than being with her for reasons of truth. And he would never let her forget that she had once declined his advances.

Beth feels guilty for thinking about Slade in a sexual way when she has far greater concerns than giving herself to him—even in her mind.

Slade gave her the most thrilling erotic surprise of her life—and the most embarrassing. But he seems aloof to her as a woman, using her blood to nourish himself then rescuing her out of obligation.

No, Slade doesn't care. Jeb does.

Jeb is also dangerously attractive. The forbidden Reflective mating is enticing.

But the Bloodlings have kindred blood. *Is that a type of soul mate among the Bloodlings?* Thinking about it all muddles her thoughts.

"Penny for your thoughts."

Beth's head jerks up, her chin leaving her fists.

"That's lame. Go hard." Jacky rolls his eyes at Maddie and turns to Beth. "We don't even *manufacture* pennies on earth anymore. They cost more to make than they're worth. How about a buck for your thoughts? Let's up the ante."

Beth smiles. The Threes lighten her. "Pay up," she quips.

Jacky gives a mock stumble, staggering backward, hand to chest. "What? Isn't my credit good? My word?"

Beth laughs, shaking her head. "Not on a bet."

"Well, that's harsh." Jacky smiles.

Maddie's lips tilt. "Is everything okay? You look kinda flushed."

Beth's hands rise to her cheeks again. Her traitorous coloring gave her away.

If only she shared the dusky Reflective complexion. Of course, now she understands why her skin is as pale as the moon, just a step away from gray. Bloodling pure gray.

She glances at her hands momentarily then meets the questions she sees in their eyes. "Merrick and Slade have located Rachett."

"That uptight dude who's in charge of the Reflectives?"

Beth bites her lip and gives a small shake of her head. "Yes, that's him."

"Okay, cool beans. So what? You're here babysitting, right?" Jacky tilts his chin up and crosses his arms.

"Yes, I guess I am. Kennet is here, too," Beth adds, trying to take the sting out of the implication that they're too immature to handle themselves.

"Maybe, but he's all wound up in talking with the Bloodlings. He's got a free pass on not getting his ass kicked, so he's 'making a study' of their species," Jacky says, using with air quotes. "Whatever. Stick a fork in me—"

"I know." Beth holds up a weary hand. "You're done."

"That's it, Jasper—you catch on fast." He winks, wagging his pointer finger at her.

Beth had a sudden thought that she was pretty sure Jeb, and Slade, would hate, but she could leave a message and finish the job.

"What are you thinking, Beth?" Maddie asks, pushing escaped tendrils of nearly black hair behind her ear.

Beth inhales deeply, taking a leap of trust. "I'm thinking that while the guys are off being heroes, we go to the lake and get you guys back to Three." Beth gives Maddie a steady look. "Chuck is dead. You could see your mom again."

My father would not pursue you, is the unspoken end to her words.

Beth could hardly blame Gunnar. Apparently, kindred bloods where as rare as Reflective soul mates, though Beth wasn't clear if their kindred held absolute equivalency to the Reflective's soul mate. Her mother had been gone for a very long time, and Beth would get the full story–he owed her that.

Beth can't see her imposing biological father with the frail young Three. Maddie is so broken.

And Gunnar is so terribly hardened.

Beth won't let Maddie be hurt anymore. She's sure that Jeb would agree with her. Taking the Threes to Papilio was a mistake.

But I can make it right.

"Hell, yes," Jacky whispers. "I'd give my left nut to get out of shapeshifter and vampire central."

"I don't think you'll have to hand that over to leave," Beth remarks dryly.

She'll miss Jacky. Something about him has added another dimension to her life.

Oh, yeah—friendship.

Maddie is conspicuously silent, taking in Beth's words, her expression melancholy. Maddie's emotional signature makes Beth's heart constrict.

"What's with the troll face?" Jacky asks.

Beth stands, dusting off her impossibly wrinkled uniform while she gains control of the mudslide of her emotions. "I was just thinking I'd miss you guys."

Jacky cocks his head. "I'll miss you to, Jasper. But I'm not gonna get all gooey and stuff."

Maddie brightens, giving him a hard poke in the ribs. "Yeah, ya are." He bends over, and a gale of guffawing laughter pierces Beth's eardrums.

Maybe the quiet will be nice, she muses.

"Don't—" Beth begins, but Jeb strides through the door.

"Don't what?" he asks.

Jacky coolly answers, "Don't forget to say bye-bye, Merrick."

Merrick scowls. "I would never leave my partner without a goodbye."

Before Beth can react, Jeb pulls her against him so tightly that she can't tell where he ends and she begins. Flesh, bone, and heat meld, and his lips hover above hers.

I shouldn't kiss him.

His hands move, one to her lower back and one to her nape. She dissolves against him, and his lips crush hers.

Beth's lost.

If he's not her soul mate—who would it be? How can something feel this right and *not* be the answer?

Her hands grip his neck, and the kiss deepens. He tastes so good that she lets the smallest moan escape. Jeb notices, and his hands tighten around her, just shy of causing pain.

"That's not a goodbye. That's an invitation," Jacky deadpans.

They break apart and Jeb ignores the boy. "I'll return."

The *for you* he left off the end of the sentence hangs between them.

Beth touches her swollen lips, never taking her eyes off Jeb. "I know."

Guilt seizes her. She doesn't reply with "I'll be here" or "I'll see you soon" because she can't lie—not to Jeb. But she cannot tell him she plans to take off in stealth—to perform part of the mission without him.

Jeb wouldn't condone her plan, but she doesn't need his approval.

Beth was Reflective before she was Jeb's declared soul mate.

The Cause calls to her first.

And Beth will answer—no matter what the price.

Jeb stares at Beth and Slade, making her feel awkward.

"Just kiss him already!" Jacky says.

Slade utterly ignores Jacky and everyone around them. He cups her face. "I do not need to kiss you, tiny frog—for you know how I feel."

Beth looks down, though his hand burns his fingerprints against her flesh.

She doesn't *want* to know how he feels. Knowing what Jeb feels is enough knowledge for a lifetime.

"Look at me," his voice rumbles at her—through her.

"No," Beth whispers.

Slade's hand clasps lightly around her forearm, and Beth's eyes move to his huge hand, which encircles her entire arm. Her pale skin is milk to the pearl gray of his.

Her pulse beats against the underside of her wrist as though searching for his lips—and his fangs.

Beth closes her eyes. Her breaths come in pants that she tries—and fails—to control.

"Stop touching me."

"Slade," Jeb says in a voice of warning, and he sounds closer than Beth likes. She doesn't want the males to fight again right before they're set to depart.

"No, tiny frog, I will *not*."

Anger infuses Beth, her face finally rising to meet his. His eyes are black gems, deep like the sea under a new moon. They glitter with raw emotion, and Beth gasps at the visual telepathy.

His hand tightens imperceptibility.

"I will not force your feelings."

Like Jeb has, she hears, though he doesn't say it.

His thumb leaves trails of fire where he strokes her jaw.

"Slade," she breathes, and his thumb crosses the threshold of her lips. The sensitive flesh trembles against his touch.

"Yes, tiny frog."

"Slade—let's go," Jeb interrupts harshly from a half-meter away.

They turn and part. Slade's fingers reluctantly trail away from her face.

Beth *wants* to kiss him; the need burns like a dark flame in the deepest part of her being.

She retreats so she won't, clasping her hands behind her back. He studies her expression, no doubt seeing her struggle, because she can't hide it. Not from him. Maybe not from Jeb. Guilt washes over her, making her ill. She sucks in a breath. "Good fortune, Slade."

His lips turn up at the corners. "And to you, Reflective Jasper."

He doesn't call her Beth or use the amphibian endearment.

Sadness bites at Beth. Some of what she feels must show on her face.

Slade stares at her silently.

Jacky and Maddie begin talking, and Jeb sighs with impatience.

But Slade ignores the others, gazing at Beth with such longing and depth of want that her lungs ache for a breath without him in it.

Beth's eyes fill with water, and finally, Slade inclines his head and turns partially away from her.

"I will come back for you." He said what Jeb did not.

And then he is gone.

Beth finds she doesn't breathe any easier in his absence.

25

Merrick

Jeb is an instinctual Reflective, though that doesn't really distinguish him. Many Reflectives are.

During sparring, Jeb was known for having an almost uncanny ability to anticipate an opponent's moves. To Jeb, they were broadcasting what would come next. He can see a strike, a kick, or anything in motion coming for a kilometer.

But anticipating Beth is another thing. Her next move might as well be a universe away from his comfort zone.

If The Cause wasn't still so firmly entrenched in the very fabric of his psyche, he would never leave her. But it is.

And what world will he take Beth back to? He has declared her as soul mate. However, Papilio is a disaster.

He must make a try for Rachett and restore order. Then he must see Beth safely home and possibly get an unheard-of waiver to accelerate her timepiece.

Of course, if she was aware of his internal deliberations, she would be angry. Beth Jasper is Reflective to the core.

Beth feels none of his angst while his travel companion dreams of killing him.

Jeb doesn't have to be instinctive to any degree to know that. He's dying inside.

Dying.

When Slade was oozing tenderness all over Beth—and she was too naïve to see through his ploys—Jeb thought he might throw up, preferably on Slade.

Certainly females of both species are in short supply on One, but why Slade would set his sights on a Reflective female who is only half-Bloodling when he can have one of his own females who is a pure blood?

Even though every fiber of his being wants to tear the Bloodling apart with his bare hands, Jeb is too smart to show how much Slade's obvious affection for Beth disturbs him.

Beth is not in soul thrall—where every thought centers first on the declared and all other needs fall after that.

He's ashamed to admit the main purpose of this venture is to stabilize his world for Beth, not for the greater good of The Cause. The greater good has faded in importance, and only Beth's perceived needs loom large.

And Jeb will not fail her.

Kennet has explicit instructions to keep alert in the short time Jeb is gone. Jeb doesn't think Ryan would jump to One. But Jeb doesn't trust One or anyone in it. He will perform this task and jump them the Hades out of here.

Slade leaps to the next platform, where his bare feet hit the solid wood, waking Jeb from his thoughts.

He backs up to the edge of the platform then sprints the three-and-a-half-meter length. He launches off the edge, pumping his legs as though he's running in midair.

He lands harder than the Bloodling did and rises slowly from his crouch.

Slade's mouth twists. "Not bad, Reflective." Slade turns and leaps to the next platform, incrementally lower than the last.

Twenty platforms later, Jeb feels as though his legs have gelled.

The final platform is six meters above ground.

Slade appears tireless.

Jeb wants to twist his head off.

The Bloodling wraps his large hands around a vine, and hugging it with his muscled body, he effortlessly slides down, arresting the speed of his descent with rhythmic tightening of his hands every half-meter.

Jeb copies his technique but falls hard on his ass at the final meter.

Slade laughs.

Jeb stands, clamping his teeth together. His legs ache, and his arms are burning from grabbing the rope of vine. His skin wears his inexperience in the raw abrasive mess of his palms.

He takes a few deep calming breaths as Slade's sarcasm pushes at him without reprieve.

Prick.

The sun is glaring, and Slade moves into the shade.

"Self-preservation, Bloodling?" Jeb asks snidely, happy at any show of the Bloodling's weakness.

Slade's eyes narrow. "One part of my ancestry is vampire, as you're aware, Jeb Merrick. Fondness for the sunlight does not come naturally, no matter the path of evolution."

"Yet you can tolerate it?"

"For the most part."

"What does *that* mean?"

Slade puts his hands on his hips. "Why does it matter?"

"It matters if you're going to suddenly be useless because I don't know what your limitations are."

They stare at each other for a full minute, neither budging.

"Bloodlings generally cannot tolerate sunlight for more than eight hours at a time. We are at full strength only at night."

Principle. "Splendid. Why didn't you convey these things beforehand?"

"You did not need to know. Those facts are not ones we blather about for public consumption."

"Why?" Jeb begins walking in the direction of Dimitri's slaver fortress. "The nightloper is no threat to you during the day. In that, you have a distinct advantage."

Slade annoyingly mirrors Jeb's gait. "True. But there are half-breed nightlopers who can run interference and scheme. That is how our females were taken," he says with quiet ferocity.

Jeb and Slade walk a kilometer in silence.

Finally, Jeb disrupts the quiet. "How?"

Slade doesn't ask to what Jeb is referring.

"After the death of my sire, I was too young in Bloodling culture to succeed the crown. So Gunnar was appointed the reigning monarch for that period before I could take the position."

They come to the edge of the forest, and Jeb feels the heat emanating from the desert. Pools of steam rise like toxic vapor above dune after dune of sand colored like pale-brown sugar.

He steps from the cool border of the woods into the scalding desert. Jeb and Slade wear white T-shirts styled like turbans, soaked in water from a nearby river that feeds the lake they'd used to jump to this sector.

Jeb feels an uncharacteristic pang of homesickness for his world.

Thoughts of Beth shove their way inside his brain.

He shoves back, determined to persevere.

"The night Gunnar was to be ordained, the night-loper's attacked."

"Beth's mother?" Jeb cocks his head, vaguely horrified because he knows Rachett's version of the story.

Slade nods. "She was caught between the two factions, and they made a show of killing her slowly, in the most inhumane and vicious way a male can hurt a female."

They're silent for a time, their feet sinking and rising as they climb one repetitious dune at a time.

A harsh exhale escapes Slade. "A great battle was waged. When one of the half-breeds spilled the knowledge of Lucinda…" Slade shakes his head, stopping for a moment. He shades his eyes against the twin suns that burn down on them, overlapping each other like bloody discs. "Gunnar lost his mind, tearing away from his command position to search for her."

"I know what happened when he found her."

Slade gives him a sharp look. "You know that Rachett discovered her first."

Jeb nods.

"In any event, Gunnar jumped with her body, and he was not heard from for over a year. When he finally showed himself, his mind was gone and Dimitri had captured all our females of breeding age in his absence. Our greatest strategist had been brought too low to perform his duties. Dimitri informed us if we imprisoned Gunnar, he would free half our females in twenty cycles."

Jeb gives a low whistle. Jeb instantly put Dimitri's real objective together: an entire generation without Bloodling births had effectively damned the species to near-extinction.

Slade nods. "It was a clever plan," he explains with reluctant admiration. "Then Dimitri became consumed with his own greed and struck a deal with Ryan while he was here for a month, receiving punishment for a crime on Ten."

Slade's eyebrows slowly rise in question, and Jeb explains. "He hurt Beth. Rachett saw to the punishment."

"Ah." Slade tips his head back, the gesture speaking to the punishment's insufficiency. "Then he did not suffer enough," Slade says in a low voice of anger.

"Agreed."

"Once Dimitri found a way to upset the balance of the Reflective sector, he was running with a new plan. Releasing Gunnar made sense."

"Please tell me Gunnar won't hurt Beth."

Slade slackens his brisk pace, turning to glare at Jeb. "What do you think we are? We are not brutes—like some."

The unspoken comparison of Reflective to Bloodling is obvious. Unfortunately, because of Ryan's behavior, Jeb can't defend his fellow Reflectives. Many were confused but still good of heart.

But a few had hearts of evil. And that was all it had taken to ruin his world. Jeb vowed to find each and every one responsible. They will suffer then die.

Slade resumes his pace. "What will happen if Beth's timepiece stops ticking, and someone other than you beckons to her?"

Jeb turns to study the other male, hating his intensity and the gall to inquire of things he knows nothing about.

He answers anyway, "I don't know."

"I *know*, Merrick," Slade says as the huge structure where the Reflectives were held for five years rises in the distance, like an ugly mirage of weathered stone.

"She'll choose, Reflective."

Jeb snorts.

"She'll choose me."

Jeb uses a clever turn of phrase he learned from Jacky. "Or she'll tell you to go fuck yourself, Slade."

Jeb brushes past him, a smile on his face. He is not normally optimistic, but he finds himself wanting to whistle a tune, especially when the Bloodling follows him in sullen silence.

26

Beth

"They are not the primitive species we have been led to believe," Kennet states, his legs planted wide, muscular arms crossed over his chest.

Beth fights the temptation to roll her eyes.

He's just a horny Reflective male, ogling the gorgeous Bloodlings.

Graceful and tall, the willowy females are delicate, in direct opposition to the males. With skin so pale gray, it could almost pass for human complexion, their deep eyes are the only features that scream their otherness. The irises are so dark that the pupil blends with the deep brown.

Oh—and the fangs.

Even those are delicate, though. Beth was glad for the curious distance the females had maintained from her.

Beth has always been one to freely state her opinion. And because she is alone with Kennet, she doesn't hold back. "You just want to have sex with a Bloodling female because all our Reflective females are no longer in close proximity to be your whores."

Kennet strides to Beth, his reaction immediate and visceral, his body trembling with rage.

"How can you presume I partook? There are many willing Papilio females who would spread their legs for a Reflective warrior."

His crass words sting Beth's ears.

"Listen to yourself, Kennet." Beth slaps the flat of her palms against his chest, and he staggers backward. "You are like the rest of the male Reflectives. We are not the gods of the universe. I've been beaten into my humility the old-fashioned way. You, Calvin, certainly Ryan, and sometimes even Jeb never see yourselves as you really are."

Kennet grabs her wrist, and Beth pops her elbow to the side, twisting hard and forcing him to loosen his grip.

"Don't even try to make me see reason by manhandling me because you don't like my words—keep your hands to yourself, Kennet."

He glares but drops his hands.

"You forget *who* I am," she reminds him.

"It's easy to do when you're slobbering all over the Bloodling instead of a Reflective warrior who has declared you."

His comment gives Beth a wicked hiccup's pause. "Even if I were, what have you been doing? Preening before the Bloodling females like a peacock?" Beth whirls away from him in disgust. "Principle help me!"

The silence is total. Only the wind can be heard beyond Kennet's borrowed tree home. The structure is tiny but accommodating—though right now, it suffocates her. Beth's eyes tear over the highly polished wood, not really seeing, as she seethes.

"Beth, I apologize."

She closes her eyes, sensing him step closer, but she remains facing away.

"Jeb asked me to watch over you. I can't condone you leaving for an expedition. What does it matter if the lake is the only surface that reflects on One? We are not set to leave until Jeb returns with Rachett."

Frustration pulls between them like taffy. Beth knows how her conduct appears. Kennet and Calvin were always fair to her, unlike many of the Reflectives.

Beth exhales softly and turns.

Kennet holds his palms away from his body in apparent supplication. "Just listen. The Bloodlings and nightlopers are the natural inhabitants of this sector. One is the most dangerous explored sector for a reason. It's heedless to run off in search of a secondary reflection. Just *wait* for Jeb and Rachett. We will depart this place together."

The lies Beth has uttered sit like carrion between them. She inhales deeply, nearly gagging on the stench of her deceit.

Just a moment more. Beth prays to Principle Kennet's attention is focused solely on her.

Her gaze remains on Kennet as Jacky sneaks up behind him. Kennet senses something and begins to turn, though Beth telegraphed nothing and Jacky was soundless in his approach.

"Kennet…" Beth calls softly, and he turns back from the weapon about to bludgeon him.

The wood comes down hard on Kennet's skull, and he crumples.

"I'm sorry," Beth finishes softly.

"That sucked," Jacky says in an ashamed voice.

Beth meets his tormented eyes. "It was the only way."

"He can kick your ass for real?" Jacky asks.

Beth remembers Ryan's viciousness in the ring, her pause speaking for her. "I couldn't take the chance. And even if I could subdue a fellow Reflective, I'd be so damaged from the effort, I'd be worthless to you and Maddie."

"You're not worthless, Beth," Maddie says quietly, a sad smile rounding the corners of her lips. She steps over Kennet's still form splayed out on the rough wood floor.

"No," she whispers, head hung low.

The Threes come to her, wrapping her in arms of solace, and Beth does something she rarely allows herself.

She sobs.

Poor Kennet is tucked underneath his cot-like bed and snoring faintly.

"See?" Jacky throws his palm toward Kennet. "He's alive and everything. Just gave the dude a love tap." He rocks back on his heels, wearing a smug expression of contentment. He flips his dark-blond hair out of his eyes and winks at Maddie. "He'll be out for the count."

Beth feels like she could puke.

She had to begin a fight she didn't believe in, knock a fellow Reflective unconscious, and sneak out like a thief in the night.

"Let's go, Beth," Maddie says.

"What about my father?" Beth asks more sharply than she intended.

Maddie's cheeks infuse with pink color.

"You're not serious, Mad? He's like—an alien or some shit. He even has the gray skin!" Jackie whisper-shouts.

Maddie's blush deepens, then her beautiful dark waterfall of hair falls forward, hiding her expression. "Yes."

"But?" Beth asks, her nausea deepening.

Her dark bluish-violet eyes flash to Beth then look away. "He told me—"

"What'd he tell ya?" Jacky asks, lightly touching her arm.

"He told me that kindred bloods are rare. They're so rare that finding your kindred blood in a lifetime is not typical."

Jacky's eyebrows rise.

"His words," Maddie says, a touch defensively.

"Well good for *him*," Jacky says with slow sarcasm. "Don't ya see, Mad? He's just trying to get in your panties and make you a Bloodling or something. You should have never given him blood."

Jacky stalks to the window and rests his forehead on the sill, gazing at the treetops.

"He'd have died," Maddie says. "I couldn't let him."

"Sorry, Beth," Jacky says without turning. "I didn't mean to put down your dad. Really."

"It's all right."

Beth doesn't want to think of the last conversation she had with her father. It didn't go well.

He wants her to remain on One and give up The Cause.

Beth can't do that.

He railed against her. Sinking low, Gunnar accused her of being selfish.

He'd lost Lucinda. How could she remove herself from the safety of her father's watch care?

Simple: Beth *is* deadly, and she is Reflective. The two are synonymous. Living on One with Gunnar as her protector wouldn't make her less Reflective—or more needy of protection.

They'd ended the conversation on bad terms. He was Beth's only family, and even *that* was a relationship she couldn't maintain.

Though she might be a proficient jumper, a skilled killer, and a just warrior of The Cause, Beth admits, if only to herself, but as Jacky would say, she blows goats at relationships.

Maddie rolls her quivering lip inside her mouth. "He won't like it if I just leave and don't say goodbye."

Jacky rolls his eyes. "God, Maddie. *Leave* the Bloodling."

Maddie sighs.

"What's more important? Some dude that professes undying soul crap and sucks your blood—no small thing—or seeing your mom again and hanging out with earth people?" He shrugs, folding his arms. "No offense, Jasper."

Beth punches gear inside her knapsack. "None taken."

Kennet lets out a low groan.

"Shit or get off the pot, Maddie," Jacky says in such a serious voice that Beth looks up from tying off the knapsack.

Maddie puffs her cheeks, blowing a stray hair out of her face. It floats to settle against her long eyelashes. She blinks. "Okay."

"Don't be mixed up, Maddie. Do it or not. But go hard."

Maddie lifts her chin defiantly. "I'll do it. I belong on Three—earth."

She looks at Beth shyly. "He's your dad, though. Are you just going to leave?"

Beth releases an exhale in a rush. "Yes."

Now isn't the time to get answers and satisfy her curiosity. There might be time for that later. Maybe.

"But—"

"Eff it, Mad. Let's go. Beth's a big girl; she can navigate her own business with Daddy Bloodling."

Jacky pulls Maddie into a hug. "Let's get the hell out of here," he whispers against her temple, and again, Beth is struck by how little of the boy is left. "I don't want to be within fifty kilometers of Reflective Kennet when he wakes up. The ass kickings will go on until forever."

Maddie giggles and looks so young in that moment that Beth's heart hurts.

Beth grabs the knapsack, sliding the pack onto her shoulders.

Bright light streams through the leaves, which are so abundant that they hardly move without strong wind, instead tossing light around like snowflakes made of the sun.

"The Bloodlings assume we're sleeping while they're down."

"Yeah, they're vamping out, in their coffins during the day, and running around at night." Jacky waggles his brows.

"They don't have coffins, Jacky," Beth says dryly, eyes skating over the descending platforms they'll traverse.

"Tomato, to-mah-to. Whatever."

Maddie silently moves beside them.

"Take my hand," Beth says. Maddie grips her hand tightly enough to cut off Beth's circulation.

Then she jumps, pulling Maddie with her.

Jacky follows. Beth gave him stern instructions not to whoop as he jumps. His *oh-damn* look made her glad she requested his silence.

Beth free falls, feeling like gravity isn't necessary.

The sadness in her heart weighs her down with each platform, assisting her jumps until she reaches the bottom.

27

Slade

Jeb Merrick is a dangerous pain in Slade's posterior, but that alone doesn't make his own treachery easier to bear.

Slade holds no joy in giving the warrior to Dimitri.

And he's unsure whether he can convince Beth that Jeb fell at Dimitri's hand. She might require proof.

Beth can never know that Slade orchestrated any part of it.

Beth is integrity driven. Slade hates to admit, even to himself, that the code of The Cause is a noble one. Even despite Ryan's debauchery, it stood the test of time immemorial. Whatever protestations he made to Merrick, The Cause had made the sectors secure and kept each world spinning more or less smoothly.

He plans to sacrifice the Reflective and gain Beth. Her timepiece might wind to a stop and reveal Jeb Merrick as her soul mate. However, if Merrick is dead, he would not stand in Slade's way.

Of course, Slade couldn't kill all who might be destiny's choice for Beth.

Slade smiles. *But I can try.*

Jeb lowers his specialized field glasses, and Slade admires the equipment the Reflectives have. It's so advanced. The bulbous tubes hold convex lenses, flicking to a magnification a hundred times more powerful than even Slade's vision can grasp in daylight. A Bloodling's vision is at near-microscopic levels after nightfall.

The short strap allows the field glasses to dangle, nearly brushing the ground as Slade and Merrick lie on their bellies behind an outcropping of boulders that blend with the transition to the non-arid topography.

"Four nightlopers," Jeb whispers.

"Species?" Slade asks, though he can almost guess.

"Lion—all."

"Makes sense."

Merrick flicks the secondary night-vision lenses over the first lenses, where it cups the bulbous shape perfectly.

"Weapons?" Slade asks.

Merrick hisses through his teeth. "Flail."

Slade gives a low chuckle. "Really?"

"Yes," Merrick answers tersely.

"Do not worry," Slade says.

"I'm not worried, Bloodling. I work a flail expertly."

Arrogant bastard. "Oh? Well then you should be primed for the avoidance of such a weapon. "Let me look through the lenses."

Merrick flips the leather cord over his neck and wordlessly hands the glasses to Slade.

Slade grips the short handgrips and presses the smooth ceramic bar to his forehead. The pressure depresses the mechanism, and the viewer comes on. The nightlopers approaching the stronghold are all oversized for the species.

The one in the forward position, directly in front of the twelve-foot solid wood doors, has a flail strapped across his body. The two lions flanking him have smaller flails. Slade studies the largest weapon's stiff rod with a ten-inch chain, ending in a metal ball covered in blunt spikes.

"Poison-tipped, most likely."

Merrick grunts a response, which Slade interprets as an affirmative.

"Do all Reflectives train for medieval weaponry?" Slade asks, genuinely curious. No matter how hard he tries, Slade can't picture Beth wielding a flail.

"Thinking of Beth, Bloodling?" Merrick asks with an intuitive stab.

Slade senses Merrick's gaze scorching his flesh, and he rattles the snake's cage.

"Always."

"She could kill any one of those nightlopers," Merrick says, and Slade hears the pride in his voice.

"Really? It must grate on you to have a warrior as a soul mate, eh, Merrick?"

"And wouldn't it bother *you* to feel as though your protection was insufficient because your declared was in a dangerous occupation?"

"My mate would not put herself in harm's way." Slade shrugs.

"*Ah*. And you *choose* your kindred blood?" Merrick makes a low disdainful noise. "Gunnar made that quite clear it is a random selection, very much like our soul mates within the Reflective contingent."

Slade says nothing, his lips tightening.

Beth is kindred blood to Slade. He tasted of her essence and gave her pleasure while he drank. That is only possible between kindred blood. It doesn't always happen, but often it does. Sexual pleasure during blood share is just one of many signs proving kindred status.

Beth will not be a warrior when she becomes my mate.

"What's that smug expression for?" Merrick asks.

You don't want to know.

"I don't think our kindred blood can be compared to your soul mate."

Merrick says nothing, flipping out his palm to receive the field glasses. Slade slaps them in his hand.

"You're presumptuous, Bloodling."

"And you, as well."

Merrick stands, ignoring Slade's rebuttal. "How are we going to do this?"

"As quietly as possible."

"How?"

Slade rummages in his knapsack and pulls out a ceramic container, which he hands to Jeb. After twisting off the top, Jeb takes an exploratory sniff.

He gags.

Slade chuckles in delight.

Merrick's gold brows drop low. "Fuck off, Bloodling."

Slade's expression sobers, but the remnants of a smile hover over his lips. "We apply that to our exposed skin, and the nightloper will interpret your stench as a common animal."

Jeb's jaw works back and forth. "Fantastic." His nose scrunches at the foul odor.

"And you?"

"I don't have a scent. My vampire lineage cancels out odor."

"Hmm." More than a hint of admiration rides the fine line of envy in Jeb's tone.

Slade ruthlessly shoves aside another pang of regret. He cannot be weak.

Merrick for Beth—it is the only solution.

Jeb reluctantly smears the foul rub onto his cheekbones and tops of his hands.

If Slade's fortunate, Merrick will take the fall, Dimitri will die, and nothing will stand in the way of his mating of Beth.

Merrick

The males go wide, Jeb several meters opposite Slade as they edge toward the front of Dimitri's fortress. Slade makes a high-pitched noise that mimics a bird call, and Jeb returns it.

The nightlopers snuffle, shaking their tawny manes and straightening from their semi-slouched positions.

The lead nightloper plucks the flail from its tether and moves silently toward a creature presumably as large as he.

Jeb jogs lightly toward the corner of the building, where he presses the side of his face against the cool stone.

The nightlopers raise their noses to the sky, nostrils flaring and sniffing the night air.

Jeb can barely tolerate the waxy substance smeared over his face and hands. He smells like spoiling refuse.

Suddenly, the leader's face whips in Jeb's direction. Jeb catches sight of Slade sprinting behind the three lions while Jeb's horrible smell serves as a distraction.

Slade's dark eyes flash at Jeb, and the second the leader is two meters away, Jeb hears a growl that tells him the nightloper has located him. He steps out, revealing himself.

The nightloper seems surprised his prey is humanoid, but the lion is cunning, nevertheless. He swings his flail in a practiced arc meant to lobe Jeb's head off.

Not today.

Jeb ducks, swinging out his arm, and grips the handle of the flail. He jerks it backward, and the sudden backswing of the spiked weapon crushes the nightloper between the eyes.

He begins to topple, and Merrick pitches forward to catch the flail as the end of another takes a chunk out of his hide. Jeb bites back a howl and spins the borrowed flail with grace, despite the pain. His strike lands between the legs of one of the others.

He howls, grabbing his ruined crotch, and Jeb strikes the second lion in the throat with the knuckles of his free hand, silencing the beast before he can rouse the entire compound.

Slade stands, blood dripping from his parted lips. He issues a primal hiss, and Jeb fights backing away, but is paradoxically fascinated by the fangs. They look as though they could belong to a small saber-toothed tiger.

"That was simple," Slade says.

"No. You used me as bait," Jeb says with clear reproach, his ass in agony.

"And if I mentioned you carried the scent of the primary predator of the nightloper?"

"I would have told you to go to hades."

Slade grins, cocking an inky eyebrow. "Ah, but look how well it worked."

Jeb wonders on that. "Let's get to Rachett."

"You go first." Slade sweeps his palm at the entrance doors a few meters away.

Jeb turns to study the huge double doors, arched at the top, anchored with hand-forged fasteners. The construction is similar to many doors on Papilio.

That is where the similarities between the two worlds end, Jeb is sure. He marches toward the entrance.

He can't wait until he is through this and back with Beth. Rachett will be reinstated, and Beth will be safe—or as safe as he can make her.

At the door, Jeb slides his fingers through the cold metal loop serving as a door knob and slowly swings open the heavy door.

The inside of the structure is how he remembers it. Yet, it is quiet like the tomb.

Too quiet.

He steps inside, feeling Slade's presence at his back. Jeb moves to ask Slade about the oddity of the building's stillness—then Reflective Ryan steps from the shadows.

Jeb's every instinct comes alive. His stomach drops as adrenaline floods him.

"Well, hello, *Jeb*."

Ryan's eyes flick to Slade. "I don't know how you managed it, my Bloodling friend, but I'm beyond happy."

Jeb's stomach flips in a hot roil. However, he allows nothing to bleed onto his countenance. No hopelessness. No fear.

I am Reflective.

Jeb's eyes narrow as he steps sideways to keep both Slade and Ryan within sight.

"I am not your friend, hopper."

Ryan smiles. "Well, you certainly aren't his." He indicates Jeb with a tilt of his head.

"What in Principle is going on?" Jeb asks.

Ryan clasps his hands behind his back, and Jeb calculates his demise in precise increments. Ryan is as intuitive as Jeb is. He must notice Jeb's study of him.

"Don't bother." He snaps his fingers, and ten nightlopers slink out of the shadows.

Jeb's odds continue to look worse.

"What's going on is we're torturing Rachett for fun. And you're going to kill Dimitri. For me."

Jeb doesn't stagger at the news but it's so close he can taste it.

With Ryan in the same sector as she is, Beth is naked without Jeb's protection.

Slade's a traitor, but he doesn't want harm to come to Beth.

"Beth!" Jeb yells at Slade as though he's lobbing a slow-pitch ball toward Slade.

"Don't worry about our Beth, Jeb," Ryan says condescendingly. "We'll take good care of her after you're gone." He gives a smooth roll of his hips, punching them out at the end of his grind.

Jeb grits his teeth. "Do not touch her." Rage makes his voice sound like a burning torch.

"Ah!" Ryan snaps his head back and smirks. "You have declared the little mongrel. Don't worry about the specifics. You can be released from that. You die; she's free. Simple." He chortles.

Jeb glares at Slade, who returns his stare with stoic indifference.

"Slade..." Jeb implores him with the one word.

"It's out of my hands, hopper."

"Even as we speak, a group of nightlopers make their way to her. She will be brought here and brought low. By me." He rubs his hands together.

Jeb's stomach churns again. "No," he grates between his teeth.

"Yes, yes, *yes*," Ryan chimes. He flicks his eyes to the nightlopers. "Take him."

Jeb doesn't honor pride; it's not the Reflective way.

But he kills half the nightlopers who lay hands on him and maims two more before Ryan wades in and beats him unconscious.

Jeb's last waking thought is of Beth.

28

Beth

Guilt hides inside Beth like an uninvited passenger as she steers her small group toward the lake. Toward Three. Toward freedom.

She didn't say goodbye to Gunnar or allow Maddie to. That would have required far too many explanations, leaving too many ways for Gunnar to convince Beth her choices were illogical.

Besides, sneaking off in broad daylight when the Bloodlings rest is infinitely easier.

"I don't like it," Maddie says, her eyes darting around at the shadows in the forest.

This last stretch of woods reveals the sparkling lake just beyond its border. Beth won't be deterred by nerves. She hops over a fallen branch, its sharp end impaling the forest floor. Skeletal secondary branches reach out like beseeching limbs preparing for an unwanted embrace.

"Creepy—I won't lie." Jacky looks around, keeping Beth's brisk pace.

"You two, quit it," Beth says, swatting the most offending branch out of the way.

The gnarled wood snaps back, seeming to cling to her tight wardrobe. All Reflectives uniforms are tight fitting. One doesn't fight hand-to-hand combat in loose clothing unless one wants it used against him as a weapon.

So says Rachett.

A somber pang races through Beth at the thought of their missing leader, and she longs for Jeb's success.

Beth takes a step forward just as Maddie's piercing scream shatters the forest's stillness.

Beth spins.

Jacky points behind Beth.

The branch is attached—and not letting go.

Enchanted wood. Beth seamlessly puts together.

Beth looks up. The tree branch is no such thing. The tree is a reverse monster of a trunk. It begins in starts and fits of slender, knotted wood, its "arms" reaching out and up until its canopy creates an end.

The branch tightens around her shoulder, and Beth moans.

"That fucking twig's a bruiser."

"Jacky, shut up." Maddie's scared eyes roll in Beth's direction, too wide for her face. All the fear that Beth does not allow herself to feel fills Maddie's gaze.

"Beth—don't move," Jacky says.

"Like I can," Beth grits her teeth.

"What—what does it want?" Maddie asks, huddling against Jacky.

"Payment," a voice that sounds like leaves falling says from far above.

"Oh shit—that sounds *bad*."

Maddie and Jacky stand together. "Listen, Jasper, I'd go all white knight and that, but I'm thinking there's no ass to kick on a tree."

Fantastic.

The "fingers" tighten around her collarbone, and Beth gasps. The pain is akin to a wench being tightened on a Three automobile far past the point of resistance.

"Reflective," the tree thing crows. Rustling leaves rake over Beth's sensitive eardrums, thrumming through her as the pain from its hold becomes unbearable.

"What?" Beth yells. "Release me then tell me what you require!"

Four horrible seconds roll past, and right before it releases her, the hold tightens.

Beth drops to her knees when the pressure of the wooden grip loosens, and she immediately throws up from the pain.

"Oh my God, Beth." Maddie moves forward.

"Stay there," Beth says then retches again. She hangs suspended over her own vomit for a moment then wipes her mouth. She spits out the vilest of her regurgitated food and rises to her feet shakily.

The tree organism's veins pulse with the emerald of the foliage all around them.

Bulbous wood stabs deeply into the ground, feeding it. The "roots" grab at the forest floor, sucking whatever is beneath directly into the creature's circulatory system. The veins stand out in stark relief against the deeply furrowed, grayish-brown bark.

"You know—" Jacky starts, and Beth holds up a hand, fighting back another urge to vomit.

She swallows her pain and fear. Beth's shoulder aches as though it were nearly torn from its socket. When her eyes reach the top of the tree, a sort of face looks back at her from above. Slowly blinking eyes regard her. Eyelashes made of leaves float softly up and down as the tree stares.

Jacky whispers, "It's like a leech. Y'know, it sucks the life out of everything."

Beth agrees.

"Be silent, male of sector Three," it commands.

Jacky slaps his hands over his ears and retreats a step.

The tree's slender neck swivels with deliberate precision toward Beth.

"Do you know what I am?" it asks Beth.

I do, and I fear you.

Beth finds her mettle. *I am Reflective.*

Her heartbeat speeds, and her palms are damp. She answers in a powerful voice, "I do. I believed your kind to be extinct," Beth adds, though it's not strictly necessary.

She's never wanted so badly for Jeb. Even traitorous longing for Slade's presence enters her mind.

During Beth's study of the sectors—and she knows the least about One—she had read of the enchanted forests and instantly dismissed their importance. So few had been reported that Beth didn't place value on the small amount of literature and merely skimmed it.

However, the pockets of magical forests were supposedly the one universal in all sectors. No matter how hard the papiliones searched, they never found one on their home world.

"We hide in plain sight, and we are few," the tree replies, seeming to grow more regal before her eyes.

"Okaaaay, that's great," Jacky begins, and Beth's peripheral vision catches Maddie elbowing him in the ribs. "Hey!"

"Shut up!" Maddie hisses.

Beth's eyes flick to the sun filtering through the clustered canopy, quickly assessing how much daylight remains. *Maybe two hours before nightfall.* She can jump them at night; the moon is waning but over half.

But night holds more danger than she might be able to escape.

Rows of teeth appear in a split of bark beneath a knothole that serves as a nose. The teeth are such a startling view that Beth recoils.

"Whoa!" Jacky hauls Maddie behind him protectively.

"You require safe passage?" it asks.

Beth nods, knowing just enough to understand that she might not survive the payment.

"Your arm."

"What? No way, Jasper. Remember what I said about the leech thing?"

"I must have permission, or the pact will not come to fruition."

Beth nods.

"Hair or blood?"

"What. The. Hell?" Jacky whispers.

"What does blood give—" Beth swallows, "Give us?"

The willowy but muscled tree looks at the two Threes and back at Beth. "Blood will buy you protection and passage." What passes for eyebrows shift high on the trunk.

Maddie gives a little moan of pure terror in the background.

Beth knows precisely how she feels.

"Hair as lovely as yours is worth only safe passage."

Jacky steps forward. "Don't hurt Jasper. You can take my blood."

"No," Beth says in a low voice of authority. "I am Reflective. I shield you, not the other way around."

"Screw the Reflective shit. Your world's a clusterfuck. Just let me help."

"I would not take blood from you, male of sector Three."

"Uh-huh," Jacky crosses his arms. "What? My blood isn't good enough?"

The tree's lips tilt, making it look as though it's smirking. Bark shavings fall to the ground.

Jacky stays where he is—a testimony to his bravery.

"No," the tree replies as though Jacky is dumb. Beth knows he's anything but. "You are male."

Beth instantly looks at where the tree's crotch would be if it were humanoid.

Maddie lets loose a hysterical giggle.

"Ah..." Jacky starts, experiencing a rare speechless pause.

"Our reproductive organs do not manifest except when mating."

"TMI. Tree humping." His hands massage his temples. "Damn." He turns to Beth. "He's all yours."

Of course he is.

"Okay, blood then."

Jacky puts his hand on her arm, his hazel eyes swimming in conviction. "How do you know woody here's gonna keep his part of the bargain?"

Their gazes lock. "I don't." She gently extracts herself from his grip and walks toward the enchanted tree.

"Where is the rest of your kind?" Beth asks, stalling the inevitable, trying to skate around her nervousness through conversation.

"Everywhere." The limbs that were so still spread wide. "We are in every sector."

Beth's eyes sweep the depth of the forest, and dozens of eyes blink open to look down at her.

She quiets her trembling through sheer will alone.

When a branch touches her arm tentatively, the feather-light caress is as insidiously eerie as it is reverent.

Beth inhales oxygen laced with her own fear.

Thorns burst from the wood, piercing her forearm. Beth gasps, instinctively jerking away, and the barbs set hard.

The burn is incredible, as though instead of taking blood, the tree being is giving some of its life force to her.

Fire whips through her veins, scorching a pathway to her heart.

Beth opens her eyes. Her blood mingles with the emerald of the forest floor that feeds the tree creatures. The shimmering colors pulse red and green then turn a brilliant violet. Like liquid fire, it races to the tree creature's heart. A burst of light changes the bark to deeply riveted opaque jewels.

"Our true form."

Leaves rustle.

"Beautiful," Maddie whispers.

"Let her go, tree dude. Right now."

"Just…one more pull."

Beth's body is a husk, and she falls where she stands. A second limb scoops her up, gently laying her on her back.

She stares up at the trees, who look down at her. Many eyes blink back at her.

The thorns retract from her body. The ground flashes around her as what Beth gave the tree is flung to the trunks of the others. Their pulsing colors are dizzyingly bright in the depths of the wood.

"Our essence will remain in you, offering you protection until you leave this sector."

Beth tries to speak—but can't.

She's so thirsty, she can't think of anything else. "What—" She swallows. "How long?"

The tree bends at what appears to be a natural waist, coming so close that Beth can smell the rich loam of his breath.

Those eyelashes, so small and lacy from his upright height, fall like palm fronds to cover Beth's body. She doesn't have the strength to shy away.

Cold wisps of leafy material glide across her arms.

"You will know our forests for the rest of your life, Beth Jasper. In every sector you jump to, there will be those of the Tree."

Beth's eyes go round and her lips part, but the tree is already rising. "You will know us, and we shall know you."

Jacky and Maddie cautiously move forward.

Beth struggles even with their help. She sways as she stands.

The sun hovers. Somehow nighttime is near—two hours have come and gone.

"Oh no," Beth says softly.

The trees rustle, and Beth's chin lifts.

The tree's eyes catch hers. "Go now. Your gift of blood will be used wisely."

Yips, snuffles, and barks float on the wind. The nightlopers are rising for the night.

"Beth!" Maddie chokes.

"Go," the tree hisses, turning to face the sounds.

Beth doesn't have to be told twice. She's still lethargic, but she doesn't have to be strong to jump. She's never had to be.

"The lake," Beth manages from between the two of them. "Run!"

But Maddie's frozen like a statue, her eyes glued on whatever pursues them.

Maddie's face rocks back with the force of Beth's slap.

"Now," Beth demands with quiet authority.

Maddie blinks, crocodile tears filling her eyes.

But they don't fall.

The trio runs. Beth brings up the rear as the two Threes sprint toward the water, which sparkles like a sea of fresh blood in the dying sun.

29

Merrick

Merrick doesn't waste time on self-recrimination. He should never have trusted the Bloodling. He went against his instincts, gambling on Slade's history of protecting Beth.

That's exactly it. Beth. Slade was protecting Beth—and ridding himself of me.

Now they have Jeb locked down.

Ryan obviously is in charge of Jeb's immediate fate. He made sure there wasn't one speck of a reflective surface, organism, or material worthy of even a skipping hop in the all-stone prison Jeb finds himself in.

He is shackled against a wall naked of anything but the bindings and stone. He tests the bindings with a jerk, and nothing gives. He licks his chapped lips and winces. They're cut and scabbed, like the rest of his body.

His powers of rejuvenation have already kicked in, but without fuel in the form of food—he can heal only at half-speed.

His mind aches for Beth, his other half. Familiar wrenching anxiety fills him.

Fucking Slade.

*Speak of the demon…*In walks Slade. The Bloodling fills the jagged stone opening. The corners of the doorway have been softened by time and wear. He folds his arms and stares at Jeb.

"Come to gloat, Bloodling?" Jeb manages, despite his parched throat.

"No. I've come to relieve your mind."

Jeb tries to laugh but only accomplishes a hoarse cough.

Slade moves forward, and Jeb tenses, though he knows he can't defend himself.

"I will not harm an injured, bound male," Slade says with clear insult in his voice.

Jeb says nothing, choosing a glare as his answer.

Slade moves in closer, and Jeb readies himself for abuse. Then a cup touches his lips.

"Poison?" Jeb asks without reproach.

Slade smirks. "Just water, Reflective."

"Why?"

Slade's eyes shift away, and he speaks to the window cut in the stone, where ceramic-coated dulled metal bars bisect the opening. "I am not without mercy."

"Right." But Jeb gulps the offered water. Cool relief sings through his system like a balm. He wets his lips. "Where's Rachett?"

Slade's face goes blank.

Instantly, Jeb intuits that the answer is terrible.

"Tell me," Jeb says, clenching his teeth.

Stepping away, Slade doesn't meet Jeb's gaze. "He cannot be saved."

What has Ryan done?

"He has been given to the nightlopers."

Jeb shuts his eyes, trying to keep raw defeat at bay. If he kept them open, there would be no way to hide the emotion from Slade.

He would see it all. Jeb's hate and his love—all of it.

Slade doesn't deserve the knowledge.

Gunnar

Gunnar lowers his head and charges into the enchanted forest. Many years have passed since he's entered this forest. He does not make the choice lightly.

However, safe passage to the lake is his—for a price.

And his daughter and kindred blood have gone this way. Their fragrance permeates the air.

Gunnar races ahead, the nightlopers closing in behind him.

The trees awaken, and their many eyes follow his progress as he tears through the underbrush.

"Blood passage!" Gunnar bellows. He sails into the air, arms raised toward the heavens.

Immediately, branches wrap him, lifting him off the ground and piercing his forearms as his feet leave the forest floor.

Gunnar sets his teeth against the pain, and his fangs punch out of his gums in response to what his body deems as an attack. Venom drips as barbs bite inside his flesh.

"Gunnar," the trees course together in instant recognition. They have tasted him before.

Then the pulling begins.

"Safe passage," he whispers as the pulse of blood leaving his body electrifies his system with their essence exchange.

"Safe passage," their feminine voices reply as one.

Seconds pass, and Gunnar opens his eyes.

"Enough!" he bellows. They get only a taste, not a bloodletting.

They drop him, and he rolls expertly to a standing position, orienting himself again.

He tenses, catching sight of Nightlopers flying through the air, long arms poised to take him down, talons extended like deadly knives of bone.

The tree nearest to Gunnar casually bats the closest golden nightloper, hurling it into another. Both are tossed to the forest's edge, where they smash against the trunk of a mundane tree.

Gunnar grabs the next nightloper and sinks his fangs into whatever body part is nearest.

Blood pours into his mouth, and Gunnar tears out his victim's jugular. He tosses aside the esophagus with a jerk of his head. It falls against the base of an enchanted tree like a discarded slick worm. Gunnar falls against the nightloper, sucking the blood from the rest of its body until its skin shrivels.

He whirls, ready to take on more, but the enchanted trees release themselves from the bed of the forest, moving with steps that pierce and shovel out the ground as they walk toward the incoming nightlopers.

Gunnar changes direction and races for the border of the forest. He throws his arms wide, and a tree catches him and heaves him to the next as though he is the baton in a relay race.

Gunnar's stomach rolls with nightloper blood and the essence of enchantment as his body swings from one tree to the next.

He has no time to contemplate, for the last tree throws him out of the woods, and Gunnar lands smoothly in a center glade just as the largest of One's two suns sets behind the mountains.

He bounds to his feet, and his chin snaps in the direction of the scent of his blood.

It does not matter that Beth eschews his protection. She is his daughter, and she shall have it, consent or no. It is his gift to her mother and to himself.

Gunnar does not bother to glance over his shoulder as he races toward them.

But his eyes meet Madeline's when she turns as though sensing his presence.

He smiles his assurance, yet she does not return it. Instead, she runs to the lake, the edge of which shines in constant invitation to the ones who can jump.

Jump if you will, my little hopper—I shall follow.

Beth

"Jasper!" Jacky screams, and Beth whirls to look at what has followed them.

Principle help me.

Gunnar is hot on their trail, but the scene behind him causes her heart to skip a beat.

Enchanted trees toss nightlopers like puppets whose strings have been severed, flinging them up so high in the darkening sky that entrails, blood, sinew, and the finer points of their bodies split like spoiled fruit when they land.

Maddie mewls in open fear behind Beth.

Principle. "Jacky," Beth says.

His eyes go wide at a sky raining nightloper bodies, but he answers with a steady voice. "Yeah."

"Get Maddie to the lake."

The need to reflect itches along Beth's nape.

Jacky's eyes flick to hers. "What about you?"

A high, keening of alarm pierces the air, and the fine hairs on Beth's body rise.

Numbers—*they're calling to more nightlopers to descend.*

A wave of longing for Jeb overwhelms Beth as her father races toward her.

"Go!" Beth bellows. Her eyes mark his progress as Jacky moves toward the shore.

Gunnar is almost to her when Beth sees the wounds like pockmark scars littering his arms.

Safe passage.

She ignores his encroachment, and the instant Jacky is shin-deep in the undulating water, Beth latches on to the reflection of the crescent of one of three moons in One's starlit sky.

She blinks, and only a soft splash signals her arrival beside Jacky.

"Holy Shee-it!" Jacky shrieks, and Maddie yelps.

"We need to go."

Gunnar snatches Beth's wrist.

Principle, he's fast. Beth narrows her eyes. "Don't make me hurt you."

Nightlopers howl.

They're close.

Gunnar's eyes snap to hers. "Do your worst, daughter of mine."

"Don't hurt him," Maddie begs.

"Oh, God," Jacky moans.

Gunnar smirks, seemingly unconcerned as enemies encroach from all corners.

Beth glowers.

The first nightloper hits the water. Its roar fills her eardrums.

"Them or me," Gunnar asks, his hold tightening on her wrist bones. Visions of jabbing, striking, and maiming him shatters her resolve.

She exhales in disgust as water splashes so close that the chilly droplets land on her.

Beth lets her eyes fill with the vision of moonlit water between herself and the thrashing nightloper.

Her gaze captures the shining image of the four of them and flings them all through the reflection with ease. Heat kisses Beth's body like a whip of scorching flame.

Fire and ice assail her everywhere, but Beth is Reflective and made to travel this path. The call of the enchanted forest of Three grows louder, and their war song on One dies away.

Involuntarily, Beth sends them to the magic forest closest to Maddie and Jacky's original quadrant.

Without a locator for return. Without her partner. And without more than the vaguest plan.

30

Slade

Slade walks out of the cell feeling somehow less for his interaction with Merrick. Merrick still rubs him the wrong way. But as they say on Three: keep your eye on the prize.

Beth is more than a prize—she is his kindred blood. Her blood calls to him like a song. The sweet sounds she made as he gave her pleasure are locked inside his head to replay.

But memories of her pleasure are insufficient.

He wants to live them with her.

Slade strides to the end of the holding-cell block and takes the wide stone steps three at a time. Footsteps of the thousands who've come before him have scooped the stone out in the middle.

Dimitri and Ryan glance up as he swings open the solid wood door into a cavernous room perhaps once used as a great commons before the nightlopers' slaying of the original inhabitants. Now it is a place of holding, war, and nefarious pursuits.

"You have reneged on your word, Bloodling."

He must tread carefully. Instead portraying his defensiveness, Slade knots his hands behind his back in contemplative false leisure. "Yes, of a sort."

Dimitri strides to Slade, who maintains his casual posture. Dimitri will not see Slade sweat. And certainly, the corrupt Reflective will not.

"Speak or be at the ready to watch the remainder of your females succumb to whatever my regiment can devise."

Rape, torture, and maiming before a certain death.

Bloodlings are not apt to perspire. But a fine sheen of sweat slicks his palms. He loosens his hands and rests them with deliberate informality on his hips. He plants his feet wide apart and folds his arms. Slade's fangs throb for release, for bloodshed.

Dimitri cocks his head. "I await an answer."

"Beth Jasper is at the Bloodling compound."

"LaRue?"

Slade nods. LaRue is the largest of the Bloodling forests. His sire's carefully cultivated prime defensible position is the lushest and the oldest forest on One.

Ryan does not even flinch. Slade will give the Reflectives their nod for the fortitude that runs in their veins. How Beth survived an upbringing alongside the likes of Lance Ryan is a constant enigma to Slade.

She will not need to survive this male any longer.

Slade watches the nightlopers, "drones" as he likes to think of them, slowly circle the three of them like dying flies.

"Back off," Slade says with a guttural command.

Dimitri raises his palm. "There is no need for threats. I cannot fathom why you did not bring the female hopper, but it is not of consequence."

Slade frowns. "Oh?"

Ryan smirks, and Slade's guts perform a slow acrobatic flip.

"I have sent my kind to see her here. An escort, if you will."

Slade's heart beat gallops, and his fangs pierce the inside of his lower lip. Slade thought Ryan had lied to work Merrick into a lather before his imprisonment.

Dimitri studies his face. "Did you presume that I was unaware of your design?"

Yes, I did. Slade behaved as though she was important only as a means to access Papilio and bring down the mighty Cause.

Dimitri shakes his head in feigned sadness. His mane shines like spun gold, catching the artificial lights inside the compound. He lifts a finger. "No." He shakes his mane back and forth. "I am very aware. You spilled much blood, Slade."

"Enough to determine a few fun facts," Ryan interjects for the first time, a smug smile rounding his lips.

Slade purposely slows his breathing into calmness, feeling the bulge of something important in the pocket of his loose pants.

His contingency plan, however horrible to consider, might be the only thing left.

A nightloper, beaten and bloody, bursts through the door and throws itself at Dimitri's feet. The huge nightloper stills then asks, "Where is the female hopper?"

Slade backs away as Ryan advances toward him.

"She has jumped, my lord."

Slade flinches in surprise.

Ryan laughs at Slade's expression.

"And you are *worthless,* Bloodling. You can't jump a puddle, find her tailwind? Nothing?" he muses.

Ryan had promised Slade the opportunity to kill Dimitri in exchange for delivering Merrick. There had been no mention of Beth.

"But *I* can," Ryan says, beating his fist against his heart. A horrible intent sweeps his features, making Slade's adrenaline surge.

Dimitri turns, looking between the two of them. "What is this treachery?"

"Shut up, nightloper." Ryan flings a metal disc at Dimitri. Serrated blades whip out as it spins then pierce Dimitri's chest.

He roars, jumping over his dying messenger to get to Ryan. Blood soaks his broad and muscled chest, coating the golden fur with rust.

"You!" he roars, and the sound beats against Slade's sensitive eardrums.

Nightlopers swarm forward to assist their leader.

This is it. Ryan has caused the promised distraction, and Dimitri knows he is betrayed.

Slade is in the perfect position to slay Dimitri and leave Merrick at Ryan's mercy.

Then he will somehow get to Beth—wherever she is.

But Slade cannot jump. Only Gunnar can. And what is the possibility that Beth has jumped from One without her father?

Zero, Slade presumes.

As the nightlopers converge against Ryan, Slade breaks from the path of least resistance. Instead of killing the obvious enemy, he sprints past the one who would take after Beth.

Ryan bellows, calling for Slade as Dimitri bleeds all over, and nightlopers descend on him.

But Slade does not listen; he flies back down the steep stone steps to Merrick's cell.

He rounds the corner as a nightloper moves to attack. Slade sweeps his fully extended fangs across its throat, and the head falls back. He shoves a body spitting blood to the side, slips on the naked stone slick with blood, and jerks the keys from the jailer's hands.

Merrick's face lifts, and Slade groans, seeing that the Reflective has taken a beating since he left.

Damn.

"Fuck off, Slade."

"I do not have time for your arrogance, Reflective."

Merrick spits a wad of blood at his feet, and Slade steps over it. He unlocks the first manacle then the second.

Merrick slumps against Slade.

Slade senses his injuries.

They are many.

But Merrick shoves him away, the one eye that is not swollen shut narrowing. "I will bring my best, if that is what you seek."

Slade ignores him, lifting the object he had been stroking like a talisman earlier.

A door above slams.

A small ribbon appears in his hand, and he yanks the mirror out of his pocket.

It had cost him a small fortune, but it was worth more than ten bars of Three gold.

"What is this?" Merrick asks reverently.

"Can you jump us?"

Merrick's disdain is clear.

Shouts and snarls float to the cell. Merrick glances behind Slade. "What the fuck is going on?"

"I need you to jump us to the lake. Beth has hopped."

Merrick's face pales. "Where? Without me?"

"She thinks you are getting Rachett."

"I can't trust you, Bloodling."

"Nor can you trust Ryan. He knows, Jeb Merrick."

Their eyes lock.

"He'll find her." Merrick holds out his hand.

The ribbon tied around his wrist, Slade hands the mirror to Merrick. "Then jump us."

Merrick stares at Slade. "I'll kill you slowly, Bloodling."

Slade nods. He would do the same. "Kill me later, but for now—let us save Beth."

Merrick's eyes jump to a point behind Slade's shoulder, and he whirls.

Ryan looms large, a flail raised and swinging. It makes a whisper's call in the sudden silence.

The cell is tight; there is no room to evade.

The swing is true, sweeping for his head in a precise arc of fluid motion.

Heat engulfs Slade, and he watches the spiked ball pass through his body as though it's happening to someone else.

Ryan opens his mouth, veins standing out on his forehead like twin pulses. And then the vision of the enraged Reflective recedes until he is the size of a seed in stone.

The Reflective winks away as Slade spins, traveling with a male who means his death.

31

Beth

Beth lands hard.

Gunnar holds her fast, his other arm around Maddie. His grip on Beth's wrist jerks her hard against his body.

Beth's breath punches out in a whoop that leaves her on the ground, in desperate need of air.

Loose clouds flow overhead like escaped cotton while Beth's lungs burn.

Jacky's face appears above her.

"Got the wind knocked outta her," he says helpfully and jerks Beth up. She staggers, her arms flailing.

Jacky beats on her back, and dots swim in front of her eyes.

Gunnar appears, his black irises swallowing the expression in them. He runs a fingertip along the side of her face, and breath eases inside her lungs.

Beth is ashamed at her weakness—that his help allowed her to breathe.

Gunnar curls a large arm around her body and holds her.

"I—" She coughs. "I can stand."

Gunnar releases her, and Beth lands on her ass. It hurts, but she feels better.

Maddie approaches and Beth instantly knows where they've landed—the woods outside of where Jacky's parents visited the grave of his dead brother, Chase.

Bright sunlight fights through the canopy to throw chunks of light around the forest floor like the pieces of a discarded puzzle.

Beth can hear the forest breathe and knows it's alive here on Three, as it was in One.

"Is this—is this an enchanted wood?" Beth manages as she stands, dusting off the seat of her pants.

"Ah—yeah. Check it."

Beth cranes her neck. Eyes spring open from tree trunks indiscernible from the rest.

"Oh Principle," Beth says, hating the tremor in her voice.

"They didn't hurt us before, Beth," Maddie says.

Beth blinks, looking at Maddie in the dim light beneath a canopy so thick that the air appears green.

Maddie doesn't fit so well within Three norms. Then she looks at Gunnar.

Beth fights her emotions then finally gives in. "I am here to return Jacky and Maddie to their home world.

That is all." Beth looks at the trees silently watching them.

Her veins surface, gently revealing themselves like cobalt lace beneath her pale skin.

She feels their hunger, the hunger of the trees. Yet they do not attack or ask for blood.

Beth gathers her courage, gazing down at her feet for an entire minute. She would give every mirror in Papilio for one minute with Jeb. She feels naked without her partner.

And Beth won't even allow herself to think of the void left behind by Slade's absence.

She chose to jump from One while the two males rescued her leader. Beth won't examine why it was so easy to do.

She lifts her chin, looking directly into Gunnar's eyes. "I know you mean well. And I thought I wanted to know who my parents were."

Beth shakes her head as Maddie rests a light hand on her shoulder. Beth turns to look at her, momentarily drowning in eyes not found in Three, but right at home in other sectors.

Gorgeous eyes like iolite gems gaze back at her. "It's okay, Beth—let it out."

"Yeah, blubber away. It's just us and the trees here," Jacky cracks.

Beth laughs. Once she starts, she can't stop.

When she begins to cry, Gunnar takes her in his arms. "I did not know there was any joy left for me—until you were revealed to me. Do not take that from me, Beth."

Beth pulls away, with a hard heart that's growing soft as the rough edges of the life she has lived to be Reflective are shaved off.

Maddie stands silently beside her.

Beth shouldn't take time for this. But she can't help herself. "Tell me about my mother."

Gunnar steps away, turning to face the woods. The trees benignly stare down at them, and Beth suppresses a shiver.

"Lucinda was on a scouting expedition to our sector and was disguised as a man." He chuckles then adds, "As though a Bloodling could not easily scent a female." His lips tilts, and Beth can see the memories of her mother play over his face. His expression darkens.

"She was taking surface samples. And of course, finding nothing that reflects. It was during a time when the great Papiliones thought they could man all the sectors through hopping alone. Back when they presumed their species to be the only one capable of jumping."

His hands fist, and the beginnings of resentment leak into his tone. "I planned to kill her. She was, after all, a Reflective, and as such, not welcome in our sector. How dare the mighty Reflectives of The Cause jump here and take samples from our world as though we are their personal lab experiment?"

"What happened?" Maddie asks. Beth gives her a sharp look, and she blushes, casting her eyes away.

"I crept closer, employing every bit of natural Bloodling stealth..."

"She made you right away," Beth guesses, and he gives a solid nod.

"She said, 'No closer, Bloodling, if you value your manhood.'"

Beth smiles.

Gunnar does, as well, cupping his testicles. "She had the flat end of her ceramic blade holding my..." He lifts himself and Jacky gives a low whistle of sympathy.

"Ouch, man."

Beth's smile fades.

"Then we looked at each other, the blade fell away, and she allowed me to touch her. I swear, I wanted only to feel what a Reflective felt like." The silence eats his words. "I did not know."

"Didn't know what?"

"What she really was." Gunnar looks at each of them, making an irritated sweep of his hair as he secures it at his nape. "Lucinda said, 'It's you.' She said it as if she'd been waiting for me there by the lake, instead of having snuck in the back door of our sector."

"Her timepiece," Beth whispers.

He nods. Flinging his hands apart and fluttering his fingers as though spreading dandelion seeds in the wind. "Gone."

"So her soul mate thingy just blew up when you showed up with all your coolness."

Gunnar's brows come together.

"Yes." Beth looks at Jacky. "If she was ticking down and her soul mate was near, there'd be no holding it back."

Gunnar gives Beth his full attention. "I did not know of this. I only knew that she was my enemy no more."

"Was she kindred blood?" Maddie asks.

Beth turns to her. Though her face flames, the girl's eyes remain steady on Gunnar.

He lifts his chin, answering her question head on. "Yes."

"How did you find that out? You give her the fang treatment?" Jacky asks, jerking a thumb toward Maddie.

"I never asked. She came to me like a lamb to the slaughter, walking right into my arms with all the trust in the world. As though…"

Beth leans forward. "As though what?"

"As though we had always been mated."

"And then you took her blood," Jacky states.

Gunnar nods.

"You got the whammy." Jacky punches his fist into his open palm, and Maddie and Beth jump at the slapping sound inside the unnaturally quiet forest.

"If you mean I knew she was my kindred blood? Immediately."

"So why didn't you know about me?" Beth asks and is proud she doesn't sound like a whiny female.

"Our mating was in secret. Lucinda's time was not at an end as a Reflective, and I could not keep her safe here—so far from reflection and so deep I would have had to hide her among my people, and with all the responsibilities of my station. We found time when we could."

"Apparently enough time," Jacky says, giving a pointed look to Beth.

Gunnar doesn't look embarrassed by Jacky's crude implications. Instead, he grins at Beth. "She had the ability to skip to whatever sector she wished. Whatever time. She obviously jumped—"

"And interfered with time." Beth pauses for a suspended moment then recites, "Twelfth: Disturb not the continuum."

Jacky wanders away, edging toward the border of where the trees give way to shrubs and a graveyard rises to a gently sloping knoll.

"I am unhappy I could not have spared you the life you lived without me. But I cannot say I am unhappy to find you now. Please forgive me for my absence. I am Bloodling. No daughter would be without her father if I were aware."

"I don't need a male's protection."

Gunnar's nostrils flare. "I offer my love, and I cannot separate that from my protection, Beth. It is what a male Bloodling is."

They stare at each other.

"I can only be honest. I miss your mother, and I hate how her life ended. I would do anything to change it, but unlike you—Bloodlings cannot skip time—only space."

A prickling sensation causes gooseflesh to rise on Beth's arms.

"Beth," Jacky says, and her head whips in his direction.

Gunnar grabs her arm. "Truce, my daughter?"

Beth can't keep blaming him—or her dead mother—because they couldn't offer something to soften the harshness of her childhood. All she can do is be grateful for her father's presence now.

Gunnar lets his hand fall, and Beth intercepts it midair. His dark eyebrows rise in surprise, and she lays his huge hand against her cheek and closes her eyes for a blissful moment of warmth.

When she opens them, his tender gaze is on her.

"Beth!"

Gunnar growls low in his throat at the intrusion as they move toward where Jacky and Maddie stand at the forest's edge.

"Is this time continuum thing, like, on purpose, or can ya just—poof—go any *time*?"

"What do you—yes. It's deliberate." Beth stands beside him, her father a solid presence at her back.

Beth gazes out into the mass of graves. The bleached headstones look like newly erupted teeth in a grassy mouth.

Maddie gasps, stepping more deeply into the shadows, and Beth's father automatically puts her behind him protectively. "What is it?" His fangs garble his speech.

Beth knows what's happened, but she can't speak. Somehow, she's broken the twelfth she so blithely recited as though it would be so beneath her to breach a directive.

"How come that prick's alive, huh?" Jacky asks Beth, accusation clear in his voice. "I mean, you guys came back and did him—didn't you?"

Beth nods a little frantically. "Yes. We—he was processed for elimination."

"He looks very alive to me," Gunnar comments with a shaking Maddie clinging to his back. "Who is that male?"

Beth gulps her shame. "Maddie's stepfather."

Gunnar steps out into the brightest part of the shadows, and Maddie plucks at his tunic. "Don't—don't go out there."

The Bloodling turns and cups her chin. "A male who has hurt my kindred blood shall not breathe another breath."

"No!" Beth shouts but too late. Her hand grabs empty air as Gunnar leaps into the meadow to go after Chuck.

And his skin starts to redden before their eyes; grotesque blisters spring to life in quarter-sized boils.

Gunnar falls to his knees, and an involuntary wail escapes his lips as his skin begins to blacken and burn.

The lone figure at the top of the hill shades his eyes from the sun, looks down at the strange sight of a man on fire, and grips his trimming shears tighter.

Maddie screams as Chuck's eyes find her.

He grins, coming straight at them.

Beth lunges forward, grabbing Gunnar's arm, and drags him backward into the safety of the shadows.

"What has happened?" he croaks, and Beth holds in a sob as half his arm sloughs away under her touch.

"Three has one sun—it's very strong," she says, rolling him over.

"Beth, figure something out!" Jacky says.

Beth watches Chuck coming and her eyes go back to Gunnar. "I'm sorry, father."

Beth stands as her father lies dying at her feet and Chuck approaches.

I'll kill him twice.

But when a shimmering rainbow appears midair Beth sucks in a breath.

Someone has followed her.

Hope sparks—Jeb has followed.

Chuck walks through the iridescent tailwind of her jump as though it's not there, his eyes set on Maddie.

Then Ryan leaps from thin air to the slight incline of emerald grass, with a lightness of step that belies the difficult landing.

His eyes find Beth as though he knew right where to look.

THE END

Reflection, book three, coming 2016!

Directives of The Cause:

First: *Right the wrong*
Second: *Bear no injustice*
Third: *Change not what must be*
Fourth: *Reflect only when unobserved*
Fifth: *Protect the young*
Sixth: *Take life only in defense of another*
Seventh: *No death is without consequence*
Eighth: *Defend those who cannot*
Ninth: *Forsake not honor, for it is all that remains*
Tenth: *Reconcile emotion for The Cause, not another*
Eleventh: *Divulge not your identity*
Twelfth: *Disturb not the continuum*
Thirteenth: *Forsake not The Cause*

Sectors:

Sector One – Nightloper/Bloodlings
Sector Three - Earth
Sector Seven - Bloodsingers
Sector Ten - Papilio
Sector Thirteen - Spheres

Unexplored Sectors:

Two
Four through Six
Eight
Nine
Eleven
Twelve

Acknowledgments

It's been since March 31, 2011, when my first book, Death Whispers, was published. I'd like to take this opportunity to thank each and every one of my readers. Without you, I would not have an audience for my work. Your support, recommendations, encouragement, and critical feedback have allowed my improvement as a writer and as a human being. Ironically, words are inadequate for expressing the depth of my gratitude. Please know how much your support has meant and will continue to mean in the future.

Thank you from the bottom of my heart.

Tamara

Dear Ones:

Danny

Cameren: Without you, there would be no books.

Thank you:

My *Readers*

Special thanks *to the following: Beth Dean Hoover and Dii for all your help and support.*

Series by Tamara Rose Blodgett:

The BLOOD Series
The DEATH Series
Lycan ALPHA CLAIM 1-6
The REFLECTION Series
The SAVAGE Series
Vampire ALPHA CLAIM 1-6

&

Marata Eros:

A Terrible Love (*New York Times* bestseller)
The DARA NICHOLS Series, 1-8
The DEMON Series
The DRUID Series
Lycan ALPHA CLAIM 1-6
The SIREN Series
The TOKEN Serial
Vampire ALPHA CLAIM 1-6
The ZOE SCOTT Series 1-8

About the Author

Tamara Rose Blodgett is the author of over fifty titles, including her *New York Times* bestselling novel, *A Terrible Love*, and the #1 international bestselling TOKEN serial, written under the pen name Marata Eros. Tamara writes a variety of dark fiction in the genres of erotica, fantasy, horror, romance, sci-fi and suspense. She lives in South Dakota with her family and enjoys interacting with her readers.

Connect with Tamara:

Never *miss a new release:*
SUBSCRIBE:http://tinyurl.com/TamaraRoseBlodgettNewsletter

BLOG: http://tamararoseblodgett.blogspot.com/

FaceBook: http://tinyurl.com/TamaraRoseBlodgettFB

Twitter: https://twitter.com/TRoseBlodgett

21527974R00173

Printed in Great Britain
by Amazon